MW01592874

Fi
In
aw
judges.

—R.G. Williscroft, President
Manuscripts International

Thanks for giving me the samples pages of
Fields of Despair...I think they are quite good.
—Donald Maass
Donald Maass Literary Agency

Thank you for sending sample chapters of
Fields of Despair. It is...exciting with a strong
character...

—Paul D. McCarthy
Simon & Schuster Consumer Group
Pocket Books Division

To Lee

Enjoy!

Hugh Ogden

Fields
of
Despair

by

Harry Vance Ryerson

DORRANCE PUBLISHING CO., INC.
PITTSBURGH, PENNSYLVANIA 15222

ISBN # 0-8059-4057-X
Printed in the United States of America

Second Printing

For information or to order additional books, please write:
Dorrance Publishing Co., Inc.
643 Smithfield Street
Pittsburgh, Pennsylvania 15222
U.S.A.

Dedication

To my wife, Hildegard, for all her support. And to our sons Peter, Gary, Andrew, and Christopher.

Chapter One
Troung

Settled between several emerald hills in a lush green valley rests a small farming village. This is the Dong Nai Valley. A slow tranquil stream flows from the hills in the west, eastward and down until it splits the village in half. In the hot and torrid dry season such as now there is no stream at all. Moisture gathered from the night in the rich black earth raises with the heat of the tropical sun to form simmering waves before your eyes as if your vision were out of focus. Palm and coconut trees fill the landscape bent by yesterday's storms and by the burden of luscious fruit. Today they remain crooked and motionless as if painted there.

Every morning at five o'clock the men of the village leave their homes and return to the land, to their crops and rice fields. Their water buffalo and oxen lead the way to the field from the habit of unbroken centuries. Laughter and the chatter of women arises from the village as they and their children dry tobacco in the sun and press rice paper in crude wooden machines. This morning the routine was broken slightly by the arrival of some thirty men. Tired men, dirty and exhausted from carrying wounded comrades on their backs. When asked why they were there they revealed that they were evading the foreigners with which they had fought last night. But this was not unusual, armed men coming into this village, because over the years these men had been here before, and men like them, and fathers and sons in this village had found refuge in other villages like this one in time past. Some of the men had never come back, and a few from here had just recently joined the resistance. The old men and the lame men cannot reveal the horrors of war to the young. War like love must be felt by experience and caressed like a virgin to be understood.

For Troung van Thuy, this was returning home. After long days and endless nights in the jungle he was home once again; perhaps for the last time to have and feel the love of Ti Ly, his wife. Troung saw his wife standing in the dirt road shading her eyes from the sun. He placed Pham, who he had been carrying on his back, under the shade of a tree. One could not tell who was the worse off as they were both covered with blood. Their skins were swollen from countless feasts made by insects upon them. They smelled like they had been living like animals in heat. Their black clothes were soaked with sweat, and lines of salt appeared on their backs and under their arms. Troung took his wife's hand and looked into her beautiful and gentle face and down over the plump curves of her breasts. They walked along the empty stream bed to their house in the west end of the village behind the schoolhouse. The schoolhouse was long since deserted as the government no longer came into this area. It was overgrown with vines and it provided a home for spiders and rodents which ate them and snakes which ate them. It stood as a symbol of government authority, and it stood deserted from disuse. On the east wall evidence of its last official function remained. The wall was pockmarked by bullets. Blood spots were gone; urine stains remained as the children used the wall for a toilet. The last official use made of the building was when the Viet Minh executed the village mayor on that wall. But that was long ago, and most of the villagers had forgotten that afternoon or the reason for it.

"You're hungry! You must eat something now."

"First I must wash and take a bath." Troung stepped around behind the house and looked into the fields and wondered when he could return home for the last time and sow his rice in the fields like his father and his father before him. Under the overhang and by the kitchen entrance was the rain barrel. He dipped water from the barrel into a large bowl. He bent down like a grasshopper and removed all his clothes except his underpants and began to wash. His wife came to the door and asked if he was going to stay home for awhile. He looked up and told her that he was the company commander now and that he must recruit more men from the village to join him.

"Who were you carrying when you entered the village?"

"Pham, the commander, but he is blind now. A bullet struck him across the face, and he will never see again. I must get him and the others to the district hospital in An Loi or we will lose them all. We have no medicine, nothing to take care of them. Besides malaria is bothering all the men again."

Ti knelt beside him and gathered up his clothes to wash them herself, and she kissed him gently on the shoulder. Troung stood up and walked into the house thinking about the men he could ask to join him in the struggle.

He sat down on the bed and watched his wife clean his clothes. His gaze turned to the rice fields and the hills beyond and he fell asleep. Ti returned from outside and began cooking rice and boiled chicken; with this completed she turned to her husband and laid down beside him. She placed her hand on his stomach and down along his resting manhood; he was asleep and she could not arouse him. So she lay there with her fragile body next to him and thought about having children so that they would be taken care of in their old age. Her mother entered the hut chewing beetle nut, her mouth stained black from the habit. She asked how he was and began making tea.

Troung awoke to find his wife beside him.

But the mother Ba was there, and it was still day so he must wait for the intimacy of night. He went to the old cabinet they had taken from the mayor's house and reached into the top for the rice wine. He slowly poured some out into a tin cup. He could feel it burn as it went down. All the days and months of separation seemed like a dream or perhaps only this was a dream. Ti brought him some rice. He had noodle soup and watercress and sugar beets and boiled chicken. He said nothing and his wife waited for him to finish eating before she ate what was left. She waited for him to speak.

"Tonight, Ti, we will stay in the village. It has been safe here for a long time. Have there been any planes in the area recently?"

"Last week there was one that flew over the village telling the people to return to the government. Our guards told the people not to listen and one of them shot at it."

"Very good, very good indeed. How many guards do you have in the village now?"

"There are nine but only four have weapons."

"It is time they come with us. I will turn over their weapons to some of the younger boys in the village and give the younger men instructions on what to do and how to protect the village in case of attack from the government or the Americans.

"They are just like the stupid French. They go out as the day begins but hide in their camps at night because the country is ours. We control everything, even some of the government officials and soldiers. In 111 Corps there is a Sergeant Major in operations that works for us. We can ambush or escape operations any time we please. We have news from the North that the Americans are tired of the War and that their people are demanding that they return home. We will drive them into the sea and the capital and the country will be ours forever. This means we will own our land. No man or government will dare take it from us. Tomorrow I will take the men to An Loi village and the district hospital. First I must go into the village and call a meeting for everyone to return from the fields. We need more men and I will get them now."

Xuyen was sitting in the marketplace enjoying a La Rue beer when Troung approached him. "How is your wife?" he asked with a smile.

Troung said, "Fine" and then continued with the subject at hand. "I want you to get all the village men here to the marketplace for a meeting. Find Quay and Roan and take them with you. We are going to get some of the men to go with us in the morning."

Nguyen van Nguyen listened to their conversation. He was the owner of the small restaurant in the marketplace. He was also the nephew of the old mayor who had been killed." Troung, the men in the village want to remain here and tend to their land. Soon it will be time to sow the rice. They have had too much war to want to go away again. The old men are telling the younger ones to stay in the village; and if they have to serve to join the local militia to guard the village from attack."

"You sound like your uncle. The men must come with us because the resistance needs them. Some day the government might feel strong enough to come here and then you would all be drafted in their army, or even worse they might kill you on the spot because none of you have government identification cards. When they take prisoners they drop them from airplanes over the sea. Your soul would never be found. You would never rest with your ancestors, or they would torture you to find out about us. They would rape your women and take away your children into camps where they would starve to death. Is that what you want, you swine?"

"Because you and your men have weapons you can say that. What can we do in our defense? Nothing! But I will speak what I believe to the people when they arrive here for the meeting."

"Because we have guns! Why you are an idiot. You are a traitor to your country. Do you think the government is any better? Why do you think your uncle was executed by the people? Because he was a landlord. He bled the people for everything that they had. He was a criminal, you bastard. He would liked to have had us all hanging by our own intestines in the sun. And you support a government of people like him!"

Nguyen turned away and walked back to

his kitchen. Perhaps with all the villagers coming he might sell more food. He was determined to tell the people not to go but to remain in the village and look after their fields. Besides all that would be left would be old men, women, and children, and they would never buy in his store. For him the war was bad for business.

Troung's three comrades were returning with the villagers. Troung knew that he could not permit someone like Nguyen to ruin his mission and his duty. He would deal with him harshly when the time came. His hatred for the man swelled up within him in a raising anger. Tension and pressure built up within his head. His legs shook with his anger. It was the same feeling you have when you hate an enemy you don't even know but you must kill him to make the feeling go away. It is waiting for that last second before an ambush before you spring the death trap when every muscle and every nerve is taut. Yes! He would deal with Nguyen van Nguyen very shortly.

"Listen to me, comrades! The resistance needs you in the final days and hours of obtaining a complete victory in the field. In the past you have given us rice and have bought bonds to support our cause. Now we ask you to give us the labor of your backs and the determination of your spirit and your will to win. The Americans are losing. The government will soon fall into your hands. Right now your fellow countrymen are only fifteen miles from the Capital. We can take it anytime, we need your help to complete our victory."

A smoky haze rose into the air as the men listened to Troung. The young boys shifted back and forth looking at each other and then the speaker. He was from their village. He could not lie to them, his own neighbors and friends.

"With all of their machines and airplanes we are still winning the war. They will never destroy our determination." His voice rose louder and louder as he felt the crowd siding with his ideas. He was letting loose the frustrations and desires of long months of war, and they were listening. Sweat began pouring down his forehead. It trickled down the long scar on his right cheek. His black eyes gleamed with the fervor of the revolutionary. His black hair glistened in the western sunlight. One hand was on the pistol on his right hip and the other pointed at the crowd. His feet apart, he looked like the part he was portraying—a leader of men. "We will take back all of the land from the invaders and their puppet government in Saigon. Their blood will flow across our land and fertilize our fields and crops. Listen to me, all of you who seek adventure with the victors. We shall all march and fight together and our victory will be glorious, and you shall all share in the final victory. Your labor will not be in vain. For the resistance shall never forget those who have fought for it and with it; but for those who hide from their responsibility, the wrath of the people shall fall upon them from this day forward. You must…"

"He is a liar. If you are dead then victory means nothing to you or to those that you will leave behind here without means of support!" Nguyen shouted as he pushed Troung aside. "You have witnessed the blood of three generations flow across our land. Nothing has changed. Those in power are for themselves. These men will be no different. When they win, they shall return here to this, and you will work for them. Do not believe these lies." Nguyen now stood in front of Troung with his back to him.

A blinding rage overcame Troung. It all returned once again. The crowd was uneasy. They were whispering among themselves. Troung could see his men on the edge of the crowd gathered there. They were now holding their weapons in their hands, and they were ready for his commands; but he need not say anything. Troung took his pistol and shoved it into the back of Nguyen's head. "On your knees, you slimy pig!" he screamed. "Do you think these people would believe you, a miserable merchant who sells bad food? A nephew of a man who the people killed because he had ideas like yours. Stay on your knees, you bastard!" he shouted.

Nguyen shook over his entire body. He relieved himself in his pants. The urine dropped onto the dirt plaza. His teeth chattered. He could not speak. The shot was loud and sharp, like the cry of a newborn baby. Nguyen's face left his body and splattered into the dirt. A dripping gray mess of blood and splintered bone remained. His hands clutched the air as he fell forward; his body continued shaking for several moments, then it lay still on the Road, a crumpled heap. A moment of history to be talked about in whispers among the huts at night. Nguyen van Nguyen was dead. There would be no more dissent from this village today or for many days to come. The crowds' faces were turned to the ground as if nothing had taken place here and as if they had seen nothing. Whatever fate now awaited them they would meet it when it came. Besides who was to say Troung had been lying. After all they all knew that the mayor had been no good and that was why he had been killed; for the good of the village. And thus they talked among themselves and wondered where time and this man would lead them, by this time tomorrow night.

And so all of those between the ages of fifteen and forty-five joined the resistance. The other men were too young or too old. Troung had twenty-seven new recruits. He instructed Roan and Xuyen to issue each man a weapon without ammunition until they were ready to leave in the morning. Quay had gotten nine more boys aged twelve to fourteen to join the local militia. Troung noticed them at the edge of the crowd. He walked over to instruct them on their new duties.

"On the approach of troops, you will fire three shots to warn the villagers of their coming. If it is a small force, ambush it with electrical mines. Otherwise retreat south to the jungle area and snipe at them with your rifles until they go away. At night slip back into the village and kill their guard. If you do this they will eventually go away. If a large force arrives with many men, send a runner to the next village and warn them, and word will reach our people in headquarters so we may attack them in force. Just remember that yours is an important job and an exciting one. The people will look up to you. You are now men. Soon you will all be able to join us and fight in our ranks. So be proud and do your job well. Pay no attention to government propaganda. They come here by plane because the people would resist them in any other way. If you know any defectors, kill their families when they leave. The government will only kill them when they use them for what they want. Remember that the Party and the people will prevail. Yours will be a glorious future. Now take that pig that lies on the road and bury him quickly before he stinks worse than he was."

Troung felt proud of himself. He had the situation well under control. He had his new men and the village would obey his wishes. The sun was setting in the west. A yellow and golden hue hovered above the landscape. Birds were finding their nests for the night. The animals were eating their hay and straw in the barns, the barns being one end of the peasants huts which were dug into the ground about four feet deep and surrounded with logs so that the huge beasts could not break out during a storm, either natural or man-made. The calves were suckling their mothers. Village dogs were running home in hopes of finding food from table scraps but they had to fight for space with the family pigs that invaded the huts for food also. Barks mixed with squeals; life then had returned to normal.

Troung took a shortcut home through some of the neighbors' homes. He passed one house and an old wrinkled man bent with age was lighting incense in the front yard. He was speaking in a low tone to his ancestors. The odor of jasmine and rose reached his nostrils, and it reminded him of his devotions as a boy. How serene and still the world now seemed. He had all but forgotten the violence just a few moments ago. Violence was a way of life now. One just had to let it pass and forget about it. Troung tripped over a piece of barbed wire that one of the families had used to surround their yard to keep the pigs at home. He swore and looked at his ankle. It felt wet. He had cut it on the wire. He was getting careless. This would never happen if he hadn't been home. It served him right. My God, he had forgotten to post sentries for the night too. He turned around and headed back to the square to find Xuyen or Roan and give them the names to pull guard during the night. Yes, he was letting important things slip his mind. It was lucky that he had cut himself.

Ti had heard the news from Ba, and she had

heard it from a neighbor that Troung had killed the nephew of the mayor this afternoon. She had heard the shot, but thought that perhaps one of the soldiers had been collecting a chicken for his dinner. Her husband must have been forced to kill Nguyen because he was the company commander now. He would not do anything that would not be good for the entire village or for the revolution. Thus she knew that her husband was justified in his actions. He was after all a very dedicated man. He never did anything for himself. He had given up the farm and home life. He had never asked for anything that the men could not have. Yes, she had no doubt that her husband was not wrong.

Ti Ly added some more wood to the stove. She must cook her husband a good dinner before he left. She would make some rice cakes and give him some brown sugar to take on his journey tomorrow. One of the old buffalo had died last week. He would enjoy some of the smoked meat for dinner. Her nimble hand chopped up some bamboo shoots for a salad and she added onion and tomatoes. She sliced a fresh pineapple and cut up some bananas with it. Some more rice was added to the black pot, and she added some coconut oil to it for flavor.

Ba had just returned from the outhouse, and she seemed to have brought back most of the flies with her into the house. She picked up a broom and began sweeping the dirt off the cracked floor to the door outside. She was still chewing her beetle nut. A crooked leg kicked one of the pigs that got in her way. It went squealing through the door, stopped, and ran back into the house.

Troung returned to his home. He was well satisfied. His men and the village would be well protected tonight. He had posted eleven sentries around the village. Tonight he could sleep without fear. No artillery barrage would suddenly engulf them because they were staying in a village.

Old Ba was sleeping in her hammock. Troung had enjoyed his wife's dinner. He took Ti to the straw mat on the bench which they used as a bed. She was not wearing a bra. When he unbuttoned her blouse her breasts popped into his hands. He squeezed them gently and bent his head down to cover them with his kisses and desire. She responded quickly. Her hands found his stomach and continued down until she could feel the strength of him. It pulsated with desire, and it raised in her hands. Troung's had found her also. In the soft forest between her legs, it was moist and warm. She kissed his ears and mouth and eyes. She was his now and forever. It had been such a long time without him. He could feel her yielding to him. They were locked in an eternal embrace—they were as one.

They didn't hear the sound of helicopters or the three warning shots of the guard immediately. Suddenly the very noises of hell broke out around them. Troung shouted for his wife to go under the tunnel in the house. He grabbed his weapons and ran out the door. The night had become day with flares in the air. Automatic fire was coming from the square into the west end of the village. Fire was being returned from three gunships in the air. Troung ran madly past the schoolhouse to reach his men in the center of town. From the north end he could see vehicle lights approaching. Quay almost ran right into him. They knelt down beside a gravestone.

"They knew we were here. We are surrounded. What can we do?"

Troung looked at his subordinate with disgust. "Fight, you idiot! Return fire for five minutes and then take all of the men into the schoolhouse. There is a tunnel under the floor in the middle room that will lead us 150 meters west, then we can turn south and go into the jungle. Go and be quick. Get the word to the men."

Troung looked to his left. One of his men was jumping into a water well and a shell went in with him. There was a muffled explosion and man and water flew back out. Men from helicopters were landing behind him about one hundred meters. He fired a burst from his carbine and ran to the square to change his orders. They must escape now.

Ti Ly did not obey her husband. She had followed him out the door soon after he had left. She wanted to be with him. She was running down the stream bed for protection. A grenade fell in front of her. Ti Ly ran past it before it exploded. The shrapnel tore into her back and legs. She fell and rolled over. Her eyes sought the stars and saw nothing. She would have no children. Her blood flowed down the path that the stream would take in a few weeks. Ti Ly was dead.

Chapter Two

Harper

Captain Hardy was a husky Negro graduate from Howard University. He played football there. Now he was the battalion S-2 intelligence officer. He was standing in front of the map board in the briefing tent. It must have been 110 degrees in there even with the side flaps up. The sun beat down on them without mercy.

"As you can see from this picto map, the stream divides Dong Hoa in half, going through the east-west axis of town. You can expect the roads to be mined. We know that there is a guerrilla squad in the village as one of our psywar ships was fired at last week. We feel certain that the remainder of B-40 is heading for this area as a stop over. We have intelligence from a defector that there is a district hospital in Hoa Loi village not far from this one. It would take B-40 about nine hours of road marching to get there with their casualties. We are being committed in Operation Big Fish to cut off this route and prevent them from reaching the hospital. They will then be forced into the open, and we will be able to wipe them out. Track vehicles can cross the rice fields with no problem. The stream bed is fordable by jeep, this being the dry season. You can expect the enemy…"

Paul Harper could not take the heat in the tent. He ducked out the opening and towards Hannaman's tent. All those towns look the same and smell the same when you are in them, he thought to himself. "Yes Lieutenant," Hannaman said. The Sergeant stood there in full combat gear and ready to go. He was lean and wiry. He had a short clipped mustache that gave him the appearance of a Mississippi boat gambler. Well, he was from Kentucky in any case. Hannaman! You could always rely on him to be ready, Harper thought to himself.

"Are the men ready? Have they been chalked up for the lift off? We will be leaving in fifteen minutes. There has been no change in the warning order."

"Yes sir—they are ready and waiting by the air strip now. Why are we going in at night? This will be the first time?"

"Lancaster and Hardy got their heads together and decided the element of surprise will catch Charlie with his pants off if he is in there in any force. Anyway Brigade must have bought the idea because we are going. The bad part of it is that we will be out of artillery range, and we can't expect air support except the initial gunships until morning. The Division is still in contact and they are getting all the air tonight."

"What if we get into a real mess? What are we going to do with them?"

"Fight it out, Sarge, just fight it out and pray for morning."

The large helicopters were waiting like large tombs in the twilight of dusk. Their huge blades blew dust and rocks everywhere. Long lines of men in combat gear waited behind them and waited for the signal that would take them to their destiny in the night. Each man, each squad, and each platoon and company had an assigned task. They stood in line like sheep, but they would go into action like wolves to the slaughter. Finally they were off.

Harper looked at the landscape below. All that could be heard were the powerful engines carrying them into the night. The land below became black devilish pools hiding danger and death in every corner. At night that land was not theirs. It belonged to the enemy. Even by day it was not safe. Reports of pacified areas was a bunch of shit. Hadn't Sergeant Knoles and Private Cooke been killed driving into a pacified hamlet? And they had been going there almost every morning to treat the sick. Christ, the VC had been waiting for them. A convoy had passed just minutes before and nothing had happened. Those dirty little slopes, he thought to himself. And they had made sure that they were dead. They had stripped the bodies, taken the equipment, and shot them both in the head. Lord, where is the justice in this war?

Just two months ago he had been in California. There was also another line to wait in. All those men in Khaki uniforms. Waiting in the dusk to be taken to Viet Nam. It was a place that should have been left in the history books. He wondered how many of those men that came over with him were now dead or lying in some hospital. They had all been individual replacements. Most of them for combat units. And poor Ottermann. He had gone through basic with him and they were shipped over together. He had stepped on a mine and lost both his legs. He finally died of blood poisoning in the hospital. What about all the others? They were all coming over, it was just a matter of time. How many men would make it back on their feet? Then there was Nichols. He was a Captain and the psy-war officer. A Harvard law graduate. He risked his neck every day flying those goddamn missions. Twice they had so many holes in the plane they had to scrap the mission. One day they would get him. What a waste. Lord protect us tonight. What if we were to get shot down now or had engine trouble. Could I lead my men to safety? Could the pilots save the craft and not crash? Did I bring both canteens of water? And so his thoughts continued as they got closer and closer to the target village waiting in the night for them all.

The helicopters came in low over the village to disgorge their human cargo. The pilots began to notice tracers looping out of the village and past their air craft. They touched down, and the men scrambled out of the craft. They could now hear and see the firing from the village. Men were everywhere and all were in the wrong place. They couldn't rush the village in a blind charge because no one knew where the other elements were.

"Hello; this is raider six, come in raider three. Come in. Do you read me? Over."

"This is three—over."

"Six—this is two. We missed our landing zone. We can't see through this brush. Can you locate us? Over."

"All stations—this is six—stay off the air; Ranger wants to know our situation. Ranger six, Raider six."

"Jewle, forget the goddamn radio and follow me. Pass the word to the men to stay low and don't go farther than the mound around the village. Shoot anything that moves!" Harper screamed. "Hannaman, Hannaman— get the platoon in line. In line dammit—in line." Firing was going on everywhere. Private Craig saw a figure running down a ravine. He aimed and fired his grenade launcher. It was right on target.

Harper was kneeling behind a bamboo thicket. Tracers were whizzing over his head. "Where are the gun ships?" The entire village was alive with VC. Jewle screamed a few yards to his left. "I am hit! I am hit! Help me! Mother, Mother, Mother." His voice pleaded in agony.

"Hunt, grab the radio and bring it over here

to me." Harper crawled along the thicket until he got a clear view of the village. Someone on the other side was firing flares. He could see men running in the village. They were all coming in his direction. He fired one clip. Then he fired another. "Hannaman. Hannaman. Where are you?" Hannaman appeared from behind him. "Listen—get the men moving toward the village or they will all get away. Who's on our flanks? I didn't notice anybody."

"Ingler is on the right, sir. But Petzel and his platoon aren't on the left. They must have dropped off in the wrong place. Captain Hardy is with the first squad. He ran into them just before I got here." They threw themselves to the ground. The gun ships were firing the mini guns. If they had been thirty yards closer to the village they would have been shot to pieces.

"Raider six—this is four-two—tell them to fire in the village. Not outside. There is a machine gun in the center of the village that has us under fire. Over."

"This is six—I acknowledge—out."

The fighting went on for about ten more minutes, then all was quiet in the village. Nothing moved. They reached the berm surrounding the village. Then it began again. This time the VCs were behind them. Mortar shells began hitting the area. A machine gun opened up again from the jungle area south of the village. Woomph! Woomph! They hit with an extreme accuracy. Then silence again. Orders were given to stay put until morning. Then they would search the village.

Harper could not take his eyes away from their faces. He wanted to probe into their thoughts, but they lay there staring into nothing—those that had faces or eyes at all. The empty cavity of a man's skull—that's what he could not erase from his mind. Paul Harper was twenty-six years old last year, but today, today he was and felt about forty-seven. He sat on the edge of a step going into the wood and grass built hut. The voices of the moaning peasants seeped out from the walls within it. A heavy smoke seemed to hang in the air. Perhaps it was the moisture of the morning and yet one could not discount the acid smell of gun powder and decaying flesh in the morning sun. The "C" ration cigarette was stale but it filtered out the other annoying smells of the area—he took a long hard drag. It gave him assurance that he was still there and that he was alive. His eyes focused through the smoke hanging in the air around his face towards the CP. Distorted cracklings filtered back through the air from the radio. Major Lancaster crouched in the shade of the jeep. Lancaster was a bastard. Always volunteering the men—keep going, keep up—screw the heat. Get the objective. So now they were here, so what! They were cut off in this rotten stinking Vietnamese village—armpit of the world.

Fred Hannaman was talking to him but the words were just registering on his mind…"The bodies, god damn it—what are we going to do with all these bodies. Shit—I found one in a water well, so we can't use their fuckin' water."

"Look Sarge, Lancaster got us here—let him figure it out."

"But Lieutenant…"

"Look, if you want to dig holes in this heat, then dig them…but me, I wait for orders. Besides someone from the 2 shop will want to search the bodies for papers."

"Didn't you hear? Captain Hardy got it taking a shit. Can you imagine that—there he was just getting comfortable and a mortar round dropped right into the crap house with him in the first barrage. All we found was his belt buckle and not a scratch on it. Man, I never want to get that short. How deep is deep, hey Lieutenant?"

"Screw off, for Christ sake!" Harper noticed that Lancaster was motioning for him to come over to the jeep. He put on his helmet and picked up his rifle and started across the square. Sergeant Minh, his interpreter, joined him as he was walking.

"Sir, the Major is having trouble with some of the peasants. They claim we killed some of their livestock and some civilians."

"Harper!"

"Yes, sir!"

"Take Sergeant Minh with you and see what all these people are complaining about. Take Sergeant Lord from the S-5 shop because he has the money to pay these people for any livestock and relatives that have been killed. They have a real racket going. They get thirty dollars for every relative that we knock off who we can't prove is VC. Pay them off for the broads and any kids under twelve that may have got it."

"Will do! Hannaman wants to know about the dead bodies. What are you planning on doing with them?"

"Harper, Brigade is going to have us burn the village. When that happens, we will just pour gas on them like the huts. So tell him to wait for a few minutes, then he can have the pleasure of it himself."

"If you say so, sir."

"Move over, Harper, I have got other things to do."

All during the night he had heard the moans and cries from the village. He could still hear them. Even the children were hostile in this village. Christ, you would think that I started the damn war

Big Sergeant Lord was resting his obesity on the edge of a water well. He had twenty-three years in service and had been on the retirement list. Then just before his time was up, he got orders for Vietnam. All he thought about was his 214 days before he was out of the war and the army. Harper wondered where he got the Coke that he was drinking.

"Come on, Sarge—you are going with us."

"Around the village to pay off the families and tell them to pack their things because we are going to burn the place to the ground."

"Do I need my weapon?"

"Yes, dammit."

At the first house an old man was waiting with a knife in front of an old cow and her calf. Both had been killed in the fighting the night before. The bodies were already covered with flies. This was going to be a lousy job.

"What's the old guy tell us, Minh?" Lord asked. "Do you want to finish this Coke Lieutenant? It's warm but I packed it in my gear. It tastes half-way decent."

"No thanks, Lord."

"Sir, the old man says that the Americans killed his animals last night. He said that there were no VC in his part of the village last night. In fact he says he didn't know that there were any VC in the village until the Americans came. He says three men came up and shot his cows, thinking they were VC in the dark."

"Tell the old man that none of our people were in the village last night. So the VC killed them by mistake, thinking they were our men."

"Lord, can you imagine that old fart standing there and lying like that. We aren't going to pay him three cents. Minh, tell the old man to get his things together because the village is going to be destroyed."

As they walked away, the flies were still feasting on the carcasses of the animals and the old man started to butcher the cattle with his knife. A fowl smell arose to greet the air as he made his first cut into the stomach of the dead calf. And to think that was going to be on somebody's table tonight. But life was still going on in the village—only the intrusion of different armed men changed the picture of the landscape.

In a small hut behind what used to be a schoolhouse, Harper, Lord, and Minh met Ba. She was holding the remains of a young woman in her arms. Her glassy eyes starred into the void of time. Minh began talking with her.

Harper noticed a bottle of rice wine on the table and picked it up. It was strong and reminded him of some of the moonshine liquor his roommate used to bring to school from Kentucky. He wondered where the man of the house was. A glistening object caught his attention on the floor. He bent down and picked it up. It was under the bench. It was a forty-five caliber bullet.

"Minh, ask her where this bullet came from."

"She said that there have been many soldiers here. Perhaps one of them left it."

"Tell her she is lying. We are the first ones in this house."

"She said men searched here early this morning. She may be telling the truth, sir. She wants to know why we killed her daughter. She was only twenty years old. She was walking in the village last night and was killed in the stream bed about fifty meters from here. The old woman doesn't want to leave the village. All of her ancestors are buried here, and she wants to remain."

"You tell her, Sergeant, that she must leave

the village. It is going to become a free-strike zone for artillery because the VC used this village for a base camp. She will die here if she doesn't come with us. Tell her that Sergeant Lord is going to give her some money for the dead girl and that we are sorry that she died. But she should have stayed home when the fighting began last night. Find out if she knows any of the guerrillas in this village and where they went."

Harper noticed a pig in the hut licking the dried blood on the dirt floor. He felt sick in his stomach and kicked it in the side. The old woman screamed. It was more a moan than a scream.

"Sir, she asks why you kicked her pig? It is all she has left."

Harper was disgusted. "Lord, give her the money and let's get out of here."

As they were leaving the hut, Harper noticed a commotion in one of the huts a few yards away. He took the safety off his rifle and started in that direction. Lord was behind him and with him was Minh. They stepped over the barbed wire fence in the yard. Craig was pointing his M-16 at a young boy.

"Sir, this kid just popped up from no where. I was just in this hut, and no one was in it. And then all of a sudden he just walks out. The only entrance is this door.

Minh asks him where he came from. Harper and Lord stepped inside the hut. It was dark inside.

"Lord, take that stool and knock a hole in

the wall so we can get some light in here."
Lord shouldered his rifle and started hacking
at the corner of the hut. Millions of angry red
ants descended upon them from the roof. Their
bite was hard and painful. Both men were slap-
ping their clothes as the ants fell upon them.

"Jesus Christ, what the hell did I do." Lord
was puffing and swearing. Finally the rays of
the sun broke through the side of the hut. Ants
were still dropping off the ceiling.

"Sir, there is some loose dirt behind that
cabinet."

"Craig, keep an eye on the kid. Minh, come
in here!" Minh entered the hut, knowing that
he was now going to be asked to descend into
a tunnel. Because he liked his employers he
did it, but he never enjoyed the job.

Lord was clearing away the loose dirt. He
found a brick that could be removed. He lifted
it up. Inside there was an opening. He took
the flashlight from his belt and shined it into
the darkness. He jumped back. "Sir, there is
something there."

Harper looked over the situation and took
a grenade off his belt. He got on his knees and
crept toward the opening. He heard a scratch-
ing sound from the tunnel. He pulled the pin
on the grenade and dropped it in the hole.

Twing...one second...woompf. Dust and
debris flew out of the hole, Minh crawled up
and pointed his BAR into the hole. He fired a
short burst—then another. He took Lord's
flashlight and began the descent.

"Harper, Harper! Why didn't you take your

radio man with you?" Lancaster shouted as he came through the door. I have been trying to find out what you have run into. God dammit, next time you take your RTO with you. Understand? Now what is going on in here."

"Well sir, Craig found this kid in here after he had been in the hut, and it had been empty. We found this tunnel. Lord heard movement, so I tossed in a grenade and then Minh let off a few rounds before he went in. He is in there now."

Lancaster smiled—perhaps they had made a real find. And he would get the credit for it. "Son of a bitch!" he yelled, as a red fire ant found his mark on Lancaster's ear.

"Sir." It was Minh in the hole, and he was coming out. "There must have been a rat down there but that is all. I found this though." He shoved out a red stock Russian AK-47 rifle. It was rusty, and the stock had been broken by the blast. He also brought out an old canteen, a pistol belt, and a hammock.

"Who do these belong to, Sergeant?" Lancaster asked.

"Sir, I believe that the boy there is part of the local guerrillas in this village."

"Bring him over to the square, and we will interrogate him. Perhaps he knows more guerillas in the village and where they are hiding. Harper, I thought your men searched this village."

"Yes, sir, they did. But they must have missed a few places."

"Get your men together now and start burning the entire village. If any of these bastards are hiding we will soon find out where. Don't forget to have Hannaman destroy the bodies. There are seventeen of them in the square now. I understand that we got one civilian last night. Include him too."

"But sir, it is a woman. She is only twenty years old. And her mother has the body."

"I don't care who it is. It is a dead body—include her with the rest. And get the people moving out of this place as quickly as possible."

"Sir, I believe that it would be better if I interrogate the prisoner here in this hut," Minh said.

"All right, Minh. But let me know immediately when you find anything out."

"Yes, sir."

Minh had lost both of his parents to the Viet Cong and his brother had also been killed. He had no love for these people. When he did get the chance to question one, he rather enjoyed it. It enabled him to take out his hatred once again. He liked to be in private with the prisoner then no questions would be asked.

"Craig!"

"Yes, sir!"

"You stay outside while I go in the hut with the prisoner and Sergeant Minh. Don't let anybody in here. Understand!"

"Yes, sir."

"Lord, you see Hannaman and pass the word to the troops about destroying the village and have Hannaman get a detail to burn the bodies."

"Okay, sir." Lord turned and walked away in the direction of the square. His entire body undulating as he walked.

Harper turned and followed the two men into the hut. He shuddered again as he remembered the man with his brains missing from his skull. He was reminded again when Minh hit the prisoner in the side of his head with his rifle butt.

The prisoner was lying on the ground. Minh kicked him in the ribs and all the while he was talking to him in a low voice. He jabbed him in the nose and blood began running down into his mouth. Still the boy said nothing. Minh asked him another question and stamped on his ankle with his heavy boot. The boy groaned with pain. Minh was working up a sweat and he spoke louder and louder until he was snarling at the prisoner. The boy held his hands to his head as he was kicked again and again. Minh took out his knife and held it at his throat. The sharp point was pressing against his Adam's apple. The boy shook with fear.

"Wait, Sergeant." Harper could not stand to see the boy suffer any more. "Let me ask him a question." Harper took his canteen and held it to the boy's lips. He drank with gratitude. Now Harper said, "How long have you been a VC?"

Minh translated and the boy answered, "One day."

"Who gave you your weapon?"

Again Minh translated and the boy answered, "Xuyen."

"How many men were there in the village?" He found out that there had been thirty-three men. "Does he know the leader?"

Minh told him that the boy said that he didn't know. But he thought that he was lying.

"Minh, we have enough information. They lost seventeen of their people last night. So their ranks are reduced by one-half. They should not be hard to locate again." Harper had Minh help him carry the prisoner back to the square. The boy was unable to walk. Hannaman met them as they were approaching the square.

"What happened to the kid?"

"He fell."

"Bullshit."

"Listen, Hannaman, I didn't have anything to do with this. You can thank our great leader for it." Harper turned to Craig and told him to burn the house they had just left.

"And just who is our great leader, Lieutenant?"

"That, Sergeant, I shall leave up to you to figure out. Minh, take the prisoner over to the CP and give him something to eat."

"Sir, the prisoner reports that there were thirty-three men in here last night. So if all the casualties were theirs, then we cut them up fairly well. He had only been working for them since yesterday. So he had short tenure

34

to be any more value than what we already have."

Lancaster looked at him, studying his subordinate with his gray eyes. "I didn't ask you for your opinion, Lieutenant. All I asked for were the facts. When I want an opinion, then you shall be one of the first to know about it. Now did anyone see the prisoner fall?"

"Yes, sir, Private Craig saw him fall also."

"Good, because I wouldn't want anyone to think otherwise. Have your men speed up the burning process. Be ready to lift out of this village in one hour."

Bob Ingler was standing on a dirt mound on the edge of the village. His shirt was off and in its place he was wearing a flack jacket. He was speaking into the radio when Harper walked up to him.

"How's it going, buddy?"

"All right, Paul. We had a slight scare when you started blasting away in that hut a while back.

"Okay, I suppose. Did you get the word that we would be pulling out of here in an hour?"

"That suits me just fine. I hope I have some mail when we get back to the base. It has been eleven days since I've heard from home. The wife is expecting, you know."

"Yeah, you told me at the club the other night. Listen, can you give me a squad of your men? We need some help and some extra Zippos to torch the village."

"Sure, man! Hey, Petrusky, bring your squad

and help Harper burn the village. If you need anything else just buzz me on the radio."

"Thanks. Say, where is Petzel? He sure got off on the wrong foot last night. The slopes probably got by our flank because he wasn't there to cover us."

"He got dropped in the wrong LZ, but the old man sent him south to that jungle area to look around. I was just monitoring his conversation on the radio to the old man. He found the mortar positions but Charlie was long gone. You know he has got nineteen days left, and they won't let him out of the field until his replacement comes. That's a raw deal if you ask me. Shit, if somebody pulls that on me, I'm going on sick call every blessed day."

"Well, ol' buddy, keep your head down. Catch you later."

"Sure." Ingler put his ear to the radio again and began listening to the radio traffic. He made a half wave with his hand and soon became engrossed in the radio again.

Harper noticed that the Vietnamese field police had just arrived in the village. He was glad that they hadn't come sooner. When they went in with the first waves of troops you could expect a lot of innocent people to die or to be cruelly interrogated. He noticed that they were rounding up the villagers in USAID trucks to be taken to a refugee camp. In their fervor for their job, it was hard to tell whether they were rounding up more villagers or personal items from the homes for their own use. What a lousy war, he thought. What a lousy war.

More than half the village was now ablaze. Hot black smoke and yellow flames licked at the sky. Soot and debris was everywhere. The crackling of the fires was all around. Slowly the village was being destroyed.

Harper took out his Zippo and touched the flame to the roof of an animal shed. The wooden and straw roof caught fire immediately. The fire began in one corner as he watched and then it seemed to leap across the entire roof as if it had a raging hunger to feed itself. The fire hissed as it engulfed the entire building. It then spread to the main part of the house. Sparks flew in the air. One spark caught fire to some religious altar in the front yard. It too became engulfed in flames.

There was a secondary explosion in the roof. A man screamed in agony and fell from the roof of the house ablaze in flames. He squirmed on the ground and continued to scream. It was eerie and horrible. Harper stood there transfixed by the horrible sight. From behind him came one shot then another and another. The man bounced once, then twice, and then he was still. Harper whirled around, gun in hand to find Minh standing there.

"My God, my God—oh dear God." That was all Harper could say.

"VC!" Minh said.

Harper looked at him and shook his head and walked away. Why did it have to be him. Why didn't he let one of his men light the roof. Why him. Why did Minh kill the poor bastard. If he had only acted quickly he could have saved the man. He could have at least put the fire out. Ten more months in this country. What else was going to happen. What other horrors awaited him in the night and during the long hot days. Why did he have to come here. To save a people from themselves? These people were no threat to his country. They couldn't storm the beaches of California in one week from now or one year, or in ten years. What were they all doing here? What had the world become? Why didn't the United Nations take an interest? Why did he in the flower of his youth end up here? Damn the politicians. Damn all of them.

While the men die and fight and die some more, they talked and talked and say nothing and do nothing. This was just another Korea. Any idiot could see that. In the end what would all this prove? That a powerful nation can crush anything and all resistance? My God—history had proved that you can never kill an idea. You must replace it with another and a better one. Killing was useless. It was stupid. But he knew that to resist meant the death of his own freedom and the death of his future and the death of those close to him by the shame he would bring to them all. He must fight for his own preservation. Not for his country or against communism, but for his own life so that at the end of this nightmare his life would be his and his alone.

"Well done, Harper," Lancaster said. "We can add one more to the total body count. That's why I had you burn the entire village.

You catch any sleepers that are just waiting for you to turn your back on them. That is one less commie to worry about the next time we are in this area. Hop in the jeep, we are going out to the rice paddy. The lift will be in, in just a few minutes."

Harper nodded his head in acknowledgment and climbed into the back of the jeep. He noticed the troops leaving the village in single files towards the rice field to the west. The field police were moving out of the village with their human cargo packed into trucks. Screaming pigs and cows and buffalo were being driven behind the trucks by small boys. A helicopter was providing air cover above for the rag-tag convoy of human misery.

Chapter Three

Roan

Roan slowly crept to the edge of the thick vegetation and watched what was happening in the village. He had just missed being discovered by the soldiers as they searched the jungle. His orders had been to stay behind and report what had happened in the village to Troung. He was at least two hundred seventy five meters from the village, but he could smell the smoke even from there. The flames and smoke rose lazily toward the sky now. Buildings were demolished, roofs were caving in, bringing the walls down with them in one inferno

Out of long habit he ducked when he heard the drone of the large helicopters pass overhead. They came in fast and landed one by one on the rice field. Long lines of men and three jeeps and a water trailer boarded the machines. With a large roar they left the ground like huge birds with a full belly. Slowly but steadily they lumbered off into the distance. Soon all was quiet. All evidence of the men and violence was gone. All but smoldering ruins of the village remained.

Roan walked out from his hiding place and headed for the village. It would be safe now. At least until night, then possibly artillery would descend upon the area searching for warm flesh, women, and children. But tonight it would find only the havoc of the day remaining.

In the entire village nothing was left standing except the schoolhouse. The walls were black from the fire and the roof had collapsed into the building. But it as a structure remained. Roan headed for it. Not for any particular reason but because he wondered why it, of all things, had remained standing. The reason, of course, was because it had been built from cement and bricks. Only the roof was thatched.

On the ground by the building there was a box of C rations that had not been opened. He bent down and picked them up. He took out his knife and broke into one of the cans. He found bread inside. In still another can there was some kind of fruit he had never had before. He drank the juice and split open the bread and placed the fruit on it. He sat on a log and began to enjoy the meal. When he had finished he was still hungry. He went to a hut and searched through the ruins. He found a burnt black pot. He took that and some rice that was spilled on the ground and added some water from his canteen and began cooking it on a burning piece of timber.

For some reason Roan felt that he was being watched. He felt a shiver go up his back. Slowly he extended his arm to the sub-machine gun at his side. In one swift movement he grabbed it and rolled over quickly to his left. In this manner he moved himself about four feet from his original position. His hand on the trigger, he brought the weapon in the firing position. There was movement in a bush just a few short yards away. Just as he was going to fire, an old woman chewing beetle nut emerged from the bush. It was old Ba. She had not left the village.

"Would you share your meal with an old woman?" she asked.

"Yes!" he replied. "I thought everyone had left the village. Is there anyone else here?"

"Just my pig," she replied. "As to the others, I don't know. They even took Ti Ly some place. Now she will never rest with her ancestors unless I find her in the ruins and bury her in her proper place."

"I would help you, old woman, but I must soon be on my way to find the company. You may come with me if you would like, and I will leave you in one of the villages along the way."

"No. I was born here, and soon I will die here. Perhaps you could help me to gather some rice and food before you leave."

"Yes. Of course I will."

Roan asked her to finish his rice and then he went off into the rest of the village in search of food for them both. He went to the center of the village where the marketplace had been standing. The stench from the still-burning bodies was overpowering. He quickly left that part of the village and headed for the north end. It was here that the police had gathered up the people. He felt sure that he could find some food here. Soon he came upon broken bags of rice that had been left behind. There was enough food for a dozen people for weeks. He quickly gathered up some and put it in his sack. He took one small cooking pot and a large knife that someone had left behind. Roan then headed for the old woman to tell her where the food could be found.

"Go to the north end of the village and you will have all the rice you need. You can live in the schoolhouse too while you stay in the village."

The old woman thanked him for his help and headed for the north end of the village. Her pig came squealing behind her. Roan wondered which would get the most to eat. He took one last look at the village and headed southwest towards An Loi and his friends.

Roan was in the hills, and he turned back to take one last look at the village. It was getting dark and fires could still be seen in the village. It was the main attraction below him. His eyes were drawn to the fire like a magnet. Only tonight it was not cooking fires. It was a fire that seemed to refuse to die for it alone stood as the symbol of a proud and simple village. As he went over the hill the flames were still flickering in his memory.

How was he going to tell Troung about his wife. That was going to be bad. Perhaps Troung would blame him. No he wouldn't do that—it certainly wasn't his fault. But then he might still blame him. Well the important thing was to get back safely without being caught. He felt he could trust the villagers along the way, but the government always had an occasional outpost. And they sometimes sent out patrols and they would always reward the people for information that would lead to his capture or that of his comrades.

It began to rain. Roan was surprised because it was early in the year for rain in this part of the country. He sought cover. He strung up his hammock between two bamboo trees and got into it and placed his ground cloth over himself. He was already wet, and he felt miserable. Soon the rain came down in torrents. The entire sky became filled with dark clouds. Moon and stars were not to be seen in the sky. Roan pulled the cloth around him for warmth and wondered how the old woman was doing and if she would recognize her daughter among all the others. He hoped she would find her and, thinking of this he fell asleep, his hammock swaying back and forth in the wind.

In the early morning hours the ants below him started stirring before Roan knew that it was time to get up. Soon they found the intruder above their nest. Roan woke up with a start, swearing. He stamped his feet on the ground but couldn't get the ants off of himself. He tore off his clothes and ran back a few feet. First he killed the ants on his head and then on the rest of his body and then he killed them individually by pinching them each separately in his clothes. That accomplished he ran back to his hammock and tore it off the tree and began to kill the ants on it and on his cloth. Once again he checked his clothes before he put them back on. Then he rolled up the rest of his things and began his journey again. When he picked up his weapon, he picked it up by the trigger guard. Again he was bitten by one last ant just waiting for him on the trigger. He jerked his hand back and the gun went off. The ants had won the battle. The shot broke the morning air. Nature came to a silent stop. Then as if nothing happened the birds and insect life began to sing again and go about their daily routine. Roan swore again and began his journey into the hills. The sun was at his back. Its warmth made him dry and feel good again.

His progress during the morning became more and more difficult as he got further into the hills above the Dong Nai valley. The hills did in fact become dense forests, and because of the location in the tropics, they were in fact lush green jungles of hell. Tall trees covered with hanging vines blocked his path at every move. Patches of bamboo became impassable, and he had to go around them. Animals and snakes lurked everywhere. Especially dangerous was the bamboo pit viper and the fer-de-lance viper. They would attack men without provocation.

Roan was glad he had found the knife because it served as a machete. He wondered how the others got through this mess of jungle. Or perhaps they were still wandering through it and only meters ahead of him. They did have some of the wounded with them. There had been a recent path cut but he lost it earlier in the morning when crossing a stream. That must have been the answer, he thought to himself. They went farther down the stream to escape this part of the jungle. Should he turn back or go on. No, he thought it best to go on,. After all hadn't he, Roan, been living in the jungle and off the land for months. Certainly. At least he would never starve to death. Again one of his feet got caught in a tangle of bush and vine. He hacked at the vines with the knife. Finally he was free again. Sweat was pouring from his entire body. The jungle was muggy and hot. His lips were parched for lack of water and his mouth was dry, leaving him with a salt taste. His own body lost so much salt that it actually burned his skin and eyes as the sweat kept pouring down his face, arms, legs, and back. The jungle blocked out the light of the sky. Everything was dim. He was attacked by insects in swarms. They came endlessly. What did they live on when he wasn't there, he wondered.

A snake! "Kill it, kill it," he screamed. He slashed at it with his knife. The blade sliced through the head of the viper. White liquid dripped from its fangs as the head fell to the earth. The rest of the body became limp and the muscles let loose from the tree; then the rest of the green body dropped to the ground. Roan shivered from the thought of being bitten. He remembered how one of the men had been bitten on the ear by a snake several weeks ago. The man had cut his own ear off immediately. But within minutes he began to shake—then he had convulsions and yellow bile came out of his mouth. He lost control of all his body functions. He screamed and moaned and then died. And it had just taken a few minutes for the entire episode.

Roan found another stream. That is he fell into one because he could not see it in the jungle. It was then that he decided to follow the water out of the jungle. Along the bank he found another bamboo patch. He began hacking away at the trunks. But they were like steel against his knife. He took his weapon and fired into the base of the small bamboo trees. The bullets splintered the wood. Again he applied his knife to the tree. Finally he was able to break off eight separate trunks in this manner. These he lashed together with jungle vines. He then had a small raft for his equipment. On this he placed his weapon and food. Roan started south in the stream.

Roan studied the branches above him for snakes. He kept one hand on his knife and the other on the raft. Slowly he made his way south, foot by foot and yard by yard.

He tripped in the slime and lost his balance. He had to let go of the raft. When he emerged from the green waters he noticed that the raft was several yards away. He swam to it. And there was sunlight again. His ancestors were protecting him. Gently he pushed the raft to the side of the bank. He unwrapped his pack and took out some rice. It was delicious. He ate a mango he picked up earlier. Somehow the scent of the fruit attracted more insects to him .They swarmed around his head. He threw the fruit away and ducked into the protection of the water. It didn't help him. When he emerged they were still there. His skin was swollen from countless bites. Roan grabbed the raft and shoved it back into the stream to escape his tormentors.

Roan wondered why he hadn't taken the road to the hospital. No one would have bothered him and the police stayed off the roads at night. He had been stupid for going into the jungle alone without any help in case of need. "How stupid...stupid...stupid!" he shouted. Only the birds answered him back.

Suddenly the stream became full of more life and the current became stronger. Roan realized that he must be heading for the Dong Nai River. He was elated with joy. It meant that when he reached it, civilization would not be far away. He struck out with his feet to get farther down the stream. And then around a bend he saw the river.

He heard voices. Quickly Roan brought his raft into the side of the stream and under the foliage. A sampan passed not twenty meters in front of him. A small boy and an old man were hauling fish. A government flag flew from the stern of the craft. It was fortunate that he got out of the way, he thought to himself. Slowly he inched his way along the shore until he reached the river itself. He pulled his raft into the tall grass on the bank. He lay down to rest. Soon he slept where he lay.

The sound of frogs aroused him from his sleep. Roan sat up. He could feel that he was dizzy. He touched his hand to his forehead and felt a cold sweat. He began to shake. It was malaria again. He must keep his body cool, he thought, and he must reach the other side of the river. An Loi was there some-where on the other side. He slipped into the cool dark waters and dragged the raft in with him. He pushed off the shore and headed into the stream. Because it was still the dry season, and because the tide was low, he was able to swim across the river. Once again he pulled himself out of the water. This time he was able to leave the raft there. With his equipment on and rifle ready. He started out again.

In a few minutes he found a road that ran parallel with the river. Roan headed south. His entire body was now flaming with fever. He felt as though he was on fire. Something in-side him kept him going into the night. He placed one foot in front of the other and then repeated the process. He felt as though he were walking in mud. His entire body wanted to quit then. But his spirit would not let it. He kept going into the night. His only thought was to place one foot in front of the other and keep moving.

At last his body gave in to its demands. He sought a tall tree beside the road and fell in a heap behind it. Sleep overcame him instantly.

Roan was awakened by the gentle touch of a young girl. He opened his eyes and wondered where he was. By instinct he grabbed for his rifle but it was gone.

"I have it," a voice said behind him.

Roan looked and saw a man of middle age with one arm holding the weapon.

"Don't be afraid," the man said. "We are with you. We noticed you as we were driving by. If we could see you then the police could if they came by here today. Come with us; we are going to An Loi. You may ride under the straw in the back of the cart."

"What about the police at the check points?" Roan asked.

"They know me and I always give them some rice wine. Besides I have helped many escape in the resistance. I fought for Uncle Ho years ago." He held up the stub of his arm, "Here, take back your weapon. I could not use it in any case."

Roan had made it back and was among friends. He got into the cart and the girl named Tuy Von covered him with straw. The old man jerked the reins of the oxen and the cart proceeded up the road to An Loi.

Chapter Four
Benjeman

"Hey you...hey you...you GI—you give me chop-chop. Okay? You...you number one. VC number ten. You give me chop-chop." Like the bamboo in the jungle and leaves in a tree, these orphan kids were everywhere, Harper thought to himself as he rode through Phu Binh and the children assaulted his jeep at every opportunity.

"Careful, Mantell, or you will hit one of the little jerks."

"Right, sir."

Dust enveloped the vehicle as it made its progress down the dirt highway. The fragrance of jasmine and flowers filled the nostrils only to be choked by dust at varying intervals. The road and the wayside were beautiful but one could not afford to stop and enjoy the beauty or the sights. Even in the day, the VC could get you on this very road. The gears of the jeep ground while they slowed up for a one-lane bridge. Only last month a major was killed on this bridge as he stopped to take a picture of the winding Dong Nai River. Harper observed the right side of the road and the rear while Mantell kept an eye on the left and on the road itself. Both had weapons on their laps. Grenades were strung on a rope across the windshield. Both weapons were ready to fire. The jeep was going at full speed now. The speedometer registered and wavered back and forth between sixty-three to sixty-seven miles per hour, depending on the incline of the road.

"How far to go, Lieutenant?"

"When you get to the junction take a right. The road goes directly into the compound. Stop at the guard house. They have Chinese mercenaries for guards. They shoot anyone who doesn't stop at the gate."

"Okay, sir."

"How long have you been in this country?"

"Just nine days, sir."

"Sorry 'bout that, Mantell. Me, I got ten more months to go. Slow down for that ox cart."

"Do you want me to stop?"

"Hell no! Never stop for nothin'. Give him the horn and pass on the shoulder."

Over the doorway it said, United States Agency for International Development. Inside there were five desks. The large desk in the rear of the office was brought from Saigon. It was ornate and the wood was sealed in black enamel and decorated in gold leaf. Behind the desk sat a fat and friendly man by the name of Peter Benjeman. He was surrounded by three beautiful secretaries and one interpreter.

Everyone liked to come here because there was always a cold beer in the cooler, which was a rarity in itself, and they all had fond hopes of getting into the pants of the secretaries either individually or in mass.

"Look at the tits on that broad!"

"Wait in the jeep, Mantell. I will be here about half an hour. If I get a call on the radio let me know."

"How do I get in their pants, Lieutenant?"

"If I knew the answer I sure as hell wouldn't tell you."

As if on cue all the secretaries began to giggle as Harper walked in the door. He looked down thinking that his fly was open and that he was hanging out. That not being amiss, he was puzzled as to what it was.

"Hi, Paul—what brings you here today as if I didn't know already. Have a beer?"

"Yeah, that sounds fine. Listen, can you send one out to my driver?"

"Sure. Wong, take the Lieutenant's driver a beer. Now before you bring messages of good tidings let me fill you in on the situation in brief. You guys destroyed that village up there and the Vietnamese have the responsibility of those 270 refugees. At least that is the case stated simply. But somewhere along the line, you people dropped the ball. At least that is what they tell me. It seems as though your people informed them of the operation but failed to mention the destruction of the village until it was already de facto or a *fait accompli*. So as it stands now they tell me that

53

they have no provisions to take care of the people."

"We were under the impression that USAID had the building materials and the food to care for these people. And now Lancaster has a hair up his ass because nothing is being done and Division is on his back. It was his idea in the first place to burn the damn place."

"Paul, we gave Major Thieu all the cement and bricks that he would need to construct the buildings. What he has done with them is another thing entirely. He has gone and built himself a swimming pool. And he tells me that he had no idea that those materials were for the refugees. The fact is that he had requested this stuff before, for a pool, and we had turned it down. My hands are tied; I can't get any more stuff from Saigon for these people. It is as simple as that. Everything I had in the warehouse here went out for that project. Everything coming in is for consignment to other projects."

"Where in the world are we going to get the things that they need? And what about all of their food. My God; when the trucks left, they had every bit of food they could take with them. But by the time they arrived at the camp there was little left. Now what about that?"

"Simple! The officials taxed every swinging dick along the way to the camp. So everybody got their cut. And nobody is complaining except the refugees, and they were all from VC territory anyway. So the attitude is frankly...so what! Now you do have one course of action open to you and that is to call on the Catholic Relief Agency. There is at this time a minor problem. The VC blew the main bridge on route thirteen last night. The only other route that is open follows the river and that is about as safe as a fly on a piss tube."

"What are we going to give them—C rations?"

"Well, I don't think that is such a bad idea. Except you would have to do it yourselves. And on a per-day basis per person. Otherwise the officials again would take their cut if they were to handle the situation. Besides one case of rations brings in fifty dollars on the black market. Now I do have some health kits in stock. And I can let you have these to pass out. They consist of soap, toothpaste, a brush, a comb, and one towel."

"When can I have the kits?"

"Right now if you would like. Now you can also get rice for these people. Go to the National Police and buy it from them. I understand that they have an ample supply."

"Do you mean to tell me that we can go to the police and buy back the food that they took from the people. You must be kidding?"

"No, I am quite serious. You might even be able to barter with them. They might take two cases of C rations per 100 pounds of sand or gravel. Now your rations are expendable. So they shouldn't be hard to get. The only trouble is that the entire operation would be illegal, and if your CID people found out…well, I don't have to explain to you what would happen. I tell you what—you get me the rations and I will arrange the trade. And for the trouble, you throw in five extra cases for me. I rather enjoy the meals."

"Well, Pete, I can't make the final decision myself. If the Major won't cover for me on the deal, then I am not going to stick my neck on the block. Now if this thing works out then we have only half of the problem licked. What about their housing? We have some salvage tents that aren't worth a damn in the heat and leak like a sieve in the rainy season. Why couldn't you give us some tin roofing material and I will obtain some lumber from the engineers or one of the civil affairs outfits. Now what do you think about that?"

"Your idea is fine except I am only authorized to give out the tin to make roofs and to repair animal pens and the like. It's not stipulated that I can use it for refugees. I tell you what. You get me some captured weapons. People keep begging for them in the rear, and I will get you the tin. Give me four or five submachine guns, a dozen rifles, three pistols, and the ammunition to boot. Then I can change the invoices on the tin and satisfy some people in Saigon that want to go home and tell big war stories."

"Holy shit, friend—I don't know if I can get all the things that you want. Our S-2 shop keeps all of that stuff and then they turn it over to the troops that captured it in the first place."

"Now listen, Paul, with that new MACV directive about personal weapons not being authorized just tell the boys it was all destroyed. You get me the weapons, and I will make it worth your while too. What do you say to that?"

"I think that this entire war and the whole situation here is the biggest god damn mess that I have ever seen in my life. But I will pass the word back and you should have an answer in a couple of days at the most."

As the men were talking the sky became dark and foreboding. Gently the rain began to fall on the countryside. Then it came more quickly and it fell in torrents. The weight of the rain sounded like drums on roof tops and on the pavement. Slowly mud puddles began to form and then small streams of water rushed down the streets, carrying garbage and mud together. People rushed off the streets for the shelter of sidewalk cafes with their over-hanging roofs. Children ran into the street to take their first bath in months, and they were followed by dirty and flea-ridden dogs.

A heavy musty odor like old socks hung in the air as the rain began to cleanse the landscape from weeks of hot and dry weather. Thunder rolled in the distance and was followed by flashes of lightning. Light went on in homes and shops as the sun disappeared from view. The rains brought the mood of impending doom to the serenity of the countryside. The rain brought life to idle rice fields and it signaled the beginning of the Viet Cong Monsoon offensive against the government and the allies.

Harper stepped out into the jeep. Within seconds he was soaked to the skin. Mantell looked as if he had been swimming for days in his clothes. There was a small puddle of water on the seat of the jeep as he got in. The only sound audible above the constant rain was the unending squeak from the radio.

"All right, Mantell, you don't have to wait for an invitation—get this hunk on the road and moving back to camp."

"Right, sir. Take the same way back, sir?"

"There is only one way back until they can open the other route and keep it open with tanks."

The jeep sent out a wake of spray as it went down the road. From a distance you could see the lights of the vehicle bounce up and down on the gutted road…little realizing the uncomfortable ride being suffered by the two occupants of the jeep. The rain hit the windshield and then cascaded over into their faces and clothes. The entire countryside was covered in dark green and seen through torrents of water. The one-lane bridge was deserted and the jeep sped over it.

Harper walked into the headquarters. Lord was monitoring the radio net. The tent leaked and Harper's field desk was wet. He found out that everyone had gone to the club for Petzel's farewell party. He found some paper and began to write a memo to Major Lancaster on his discussion with USAID concerning the refugee problem. He thought better of it and decided to brief the major in person.

"Lord, I am going to my tent and then I will be at the club if anyone comes looking for me."

"Okay, sir. You look like a drowned rat, Lieutenant."

"That is precisely the reason I am going to my tent… to get some dry clothes on before I catch the Asian flu."

By this time, every foot of ground had become quires of miserable mud. Boots got stuck, jeeps got stuck, and tanks would get stuck. Harper struggled along between bunkers, tents, and buildings. He noticed with chagrin that their tent had collapsed in one corner. One of the tent pegs had come loose and the water had formed a pocket on the tent roof…thus the entire side had fallen in.

Wardell had taken the worst of the rain in the side that had failed in, Harper noticed. The tent flaps, too, must have been up during the beginning of the storm because every corner of the tent was wet. His clothes were all damp and some were soaked. His sheets and bed were one soggy mess. He picked up a towel and wrung the water out of it and began to wipe himself off. It was a struggle to get off the wet fatigues. The wet laces on his boots were stuck so he cut them loose with his knife. Being free of his clothes he grabbed his soap and stepped out into the rain to have a fresh shower behind the tent. He bent down and replaced the tent peg in the hole and pulled the drawstring up tight. The side of the tent rose up again. This being accomplished he began to wash.

"Who are you, Lady Godiva or Mr. Clean?"

"Hey, Wardell, have you got a surprise."

"Nothing would ever surprise me here, buddy. Why aren't you at the farewell party for Petzel? Everyone is half on their ass already."

"As soon as I clean up, I'm going over."

"Fat Benjeman is there with his girls. He just got there when I left. They surrounded those bitches like they were all in heat. And Petzel brought over two girls from the strip...let's see...number thirty-one, the one Vogel has been laying, and number twelve. I think she is a new addition to the forest over there."

"Was Lancaster there when you left?"

"He was there loud and clear. He and Benjeman were getting their ugly heads together just as I walked out the door. One of them was talking about weapons."

"Well that saves me the trouble of giving a briefing to him then. Would you know what happened to that care package that I got from home and opened the other day?"

"Sure—the rats got into it. So I tossed it away. Sorry but I forgot to tell you about it. Doc tells me that he found a rat in his bed with him the other night. It seems that he took a sandwich to bed and the rat must have smelled the crumbs. He wasn't sure who was more scared, him or the rat when he piled out of the bunk. He tore down the mosquito net and all trying to beat the rat out."

"Well, as long as there are rats in here, there

are no snakes and that suits me just fine. It's when the rats leave or start squealing then I begin to worry about what else we got for company."

The rhythmic notes of a band filtered out through the bamboo curtains of the officer's club. The only lights on were for the bartender—Sergeant Stewart. The card table was busy. Five men were hunched over their cards. The game was table stakes. Junior officers were invited but must have found that they could not afford the game after a few hands. There was a sign over the bar saying, "He who wears his hat in here buys the house a round of cheer." There were five men and three girls sitting on the couch. The girls were giggling and the men were motioning to each other to beat it because they thought that they had the in with the girls. A warrant officer and one girl were undulating loin to loin on the dance floor to the tune on the jukebox. All the slot machines were engaged and the coins flowed in but few came out again. Petzel was engaged in conversation and his favorite subject…that being the only book he had ever read and some even doubted if he had read that.

"I tell you in the Rise and Fall of the Third Reich it is obvious that Rommel was the greatest General to ever have command of troops. Now in ranger school, we had perhaps better training than his officers and men, but I tell you he was the best damn General that ever lived. He would have ended this war in one year. You can bet on it. Hey, Harper, come here and give us your opinion on what I am saying. As an airborne ranger, I can tell you that I would have followed that man anywhere. Of course the trouble with the Germans was that they had nothing but blind obedience. That's why they lost the war. We should have been on their side and we wouldn't be in this mess now. Right, Harper?" He shoved Harper a scotch.

"Well, I can't say that I ascertained what you have just mentioned from the book. Rommel was a great General but that doesn't mean that he would have been worth a tinkers damn in this war. Now I believe that..."

"Are you calling me a liar? I can't believe that a man like you with a college education could be so stupid. I don't want any grand opinions—I just want to know if I am right or not and in plain English. Carl, have you ever jumped from a plane? Boy, that is the greatest feeling in the world. I am putting in for special forces when I get back to the States. Now there is a great outfit."

"If they had done their job in the first place we wouldn't be here now, Petzel."

"You know, Carl, you can always tell those ROTC graduates. The army doesn't need intellectuals. What we need is blind obedience. Our country first and right or wrong it's our country. Do you agree with that, Harper?"

"Listen, I would like to talk to you some more, but I promised one of those girls a dance. So we can continue this conversation later. Thanks for the drink."

Harper walked away not wanting to start another argument again on the same subject. Petzel was only a high school graduate. He had entered the army when he was seventeen and had worked his way up through the ranks until he had attended OCS and got his commission. Army regulations he could quote from memory. But that was the extent of his knowledge. For this type of individual, the army was a way of life and the only kind of life that he knew. You could never talk and reason with these kind of people. The more you say in your defense the more they are convinced that you are wrong. Yes, it was fruitless and pointless to argue with him. Even if he won an argument then you only create hatred and animosity in the other person. No, it wasn't worth the effort, he thought to himself.

"Harper, come over here a minute!" It was Lancaster.

"Yes, sir, what seems to be the problem, sir?"

"I have been talking to Benjeman here and he tells me that he can give us a hand with the refugees. Of course he expects a small favor from us. You see to it that he gets what he needs. Do you have any questions?

"Just what is everything, sir?"

"Everything that you discussed this afternoon when you paid him a visit. And don't worry, I will back you up in case there are any questions raised on this thing. But there will be no questions because Division wants the job done and they don't give a damn how it is done, as long as we take care of it. The sooner it is done, the sooner they will forget about it and then we will turn over the entire thing to the Vietnamese. Then if something happens to those people it will be their fault entirely and we are off the hook. Now get over to the S-4 shop and talk to Hardy's replacement and tell him that I sent you. You get those items and put them in the back of Benjeman's jeep tonight."

"All right, sir, I will get Sergeant Hannaman now and have him give me a hand with all of the items."

"Fine—that will be fine."

Harper turned and walked out the door. It had stopped raining. The sky was dark and void of stars. He sloshed through the mud and headed towards the operations center to find the new S-2 and explain the situation to him.

Chapter Five
Captain Tinh

A round and full moon hovered in a star-filled sky. Occasional clouds swept past in front of its nocturnal rays, casting strange shadows on the surface of the earth. Tall palm trees swayed back and forth in gentle winds that whispered in the leaves and grass made rustling sounds in the night.

The current of the river made gentle rushing noises along the banks as it washed against the wooden supports of the bridge on route one. A leaf was floating on the current of the water and it carried a small worm that would one day become a butterfly. Slowly it flowed south and to a destination it knew not where.

Along the far shore of the riverbank across from the bridge there were five reeds protruding from the water. The water swirled around then and passed on. Underneath the reeds were five men waiting for a signal to surface and grab their weapons on the riverbank.

The road had heavy vegetation along both sides of it and along the part that followed the shores of the river for a short way. Men could hide in the thickets and bushes and reach out and touch a passerby on this road. At the north end of the bridge there was a small guardhouse. By day the two men in it come out and sat on the bridge and watched the traffic go by, waved to an occasional friend, and smoked. At night they surrounded themselves with barbed wire, cement, and sandbags. They took turns peering into the night. Their hands followed their eyes and in their hands they held a carbine or machine gun. And the eye of the barrel pointed and looked with them as if a watchdog, guaranteeing their safety and survival. You could tell they were there by the occasional flash of a match or the deep red glow of a cigarette silhouetting their faces and position.

If one could be detached from the situation they would have noticed a woman approach the guardhouse and speak a few words and finally gain admittance to it. She had been carrying food. Behind her had come three men. They had come quietly and quickly. Looking in the sentry box through the window...you could see the food overturned on the floor. One man was slumped on a chair. His body was tilted one way, while his neck hung in the opposite direction. There was a large red mark on his throat and the red continued down to his shirt and then to the floor. The other man was in his hammock. Both hands were holding on to the hilt of the dagger in his chest. His face was distorted in a permanent scream that he never uttered. A cigarette was still burning on the floor beside his hammock. The young woman was sitting on the floor. She was resting against a table leg. There were no signs of violence on her person…no blood. Her eyes bulged in a state of terror. It was then that you could notice the thin wire around her neck.

The three men that had entered had left just as quickly and quietly. They slipped back into the vegetation along the road. All was quiet. The night was briefly interrupted by the sound of a rifle bolt being drawn back and the click of a safety button as it went to the fire position.

A shadowy figure stepped from the bank of the river into the water. He wore fatigues dyed black. He reached into the dark water and pulled up one of the reeds. In a few seconds the six men left the river and walked along the shore, keeping in the shadows of the night.

Roan looked at one of the men and told him, "Place the explosives under the center of the bridge." Turning again he addressed two of the others. "Put one claymore mine at each end of the bridge and face them towards the center."

Two men slipped into the water and swam towards the center of the bridge. They wrapped each center pole with detonating cord and placed plastic explosives over that. They ran the fuse wires to the electric battery on the bridge. At the same time one man at each end of the bridge set up his claymore mine. After a few minutes the job was finished.

"Run the wires into the sentry house." The six men then entered the hut. They dragged out the bodies and placed them on the weeds along the river and out of sight of travelers on the road. Roan and two others stayed in the bunker. The other three disappeared on the other side of the road and joined the waiting guerillas.

A man in a Lambretta scooter appeared on the road. He neared the bridge and was soon over it. Nothing happened. Everything looked normal. It would be a perfect ambush.

Roan sat back an waited. Patience was his virtue. He wondered when he would have the opportunity to tell Troung about his wife being dead. When he had first arrived at the hospital it hadn't been the right time. Troung had lost six of his wounded men, including Pham, that night in the village, not to mention four of his regulars and seven of the new volunteers. Troung had been in a bad mood for days, blaming himself for the losses. The small underground hospital had been filled with causalities. The thirty beds that they had hadn't been enough. Another unit had also been resting there. Everyday there were artillery strikes in the area. But so far none had hit the tunnel complex directly.

He thought about his father who died several years ago. His family was Cao Die and had fought the Communist, the French, and the South Vietnamese government. His father had sent him to Nha Trang to the Pasteur Institute to study medicine. And that's when his troubles began. As a boy he had known French because his father was a rubber planter in Tay Ninh Province near the big mountain. He grew up under French influence and had resisted it. When he was at school the French killed his father because he fought against them. When he was at the Institute he was asked to translate papers for a professor into French. In his studies he had learned some English too. Finally in 1963, a professor confided to him that he worked for the Viet Cong. He convinced Roan that his services would be of value. One thing led to another until one day he was in too deep to get out. Shortly after that, the Party decided because of his Cao Die background he couldn't be trusted in intelligence work so they put him in B-40, a regional force company. Roan hoped that the war would end soon so that he could go back to school and study medicine again.

He was upset with himself for not telling Troung about his wife before this. But in reality he was afraid to do so. Troung in his anger or sorrow might perhaps kill him without giving it a second thought until it was over. Perhaps tonight, if everything went well after the operation, it would be a good opportunity.

Xuyen and Hinh were observing the road as Roan sat in the chair thinking about his past.

"Do you think he will make the trip tonight?" Hinh asked.

"He will come. Every night he stays late at the refugee camp and passes here about nine o'clock. Our agent in the camp got word to

Troung yesterday. This is one District Chief who will not persecute the people again," Roan said.

There was rice in the pot on the floor. Roan picked it up with a wooden spoon and began eating the rice.

"There is a vehicle coming," Hinh said.

Roan put the rice down, got his rifle, and walked to the door of the bunker.

"It's coming from the wrong direction. Relax. Troung will fire the first shot because he will see him first."

Troung peered down the darkness of the road. His knuckles were white as he gripped the rifle. His eyes observed the darkness, but his mind was wandering from one thought to the next. It was this district chief—Captain Tinh—who had taken his wife and all the others away. He hadn't even protested the burning of the village. They should have stayed there and counter-attacked again with mortars. But they were terribly outnumbered for a major engagement with the enemy. Besides his orders were to get his men to the hospital for a needed rest.

A small spider crawled down his sleeve as he lay among the plants and vegetation on the ground. It dropped from his sleeve to the rifle barrel. It was connected to both places by the first strand of its web. Troung took his thumb and crushed it on the wooden rifle stock. Crickets were chirping all around. Small flying insects and fleas were landing on his flesh and biting him. He resisted staunchly to the casual observer. He did not in fact even notice the nuisance until one of the insects flew into his eye. He swore quietly and wiped the tears away from his face.

Once again his thoughts turned to the man for whom they lay in wait. Once again his anger made his temples throb. He felt the pressure of anxiety and the excitement of waiting, like the hunter stalking his game and baiting the salt lick. They all waited for one particular jeep and one special quarry.

Like a rabbit scared the jeep started with a jolt and flew into the darkness and shadows of the lurking night. In the rear seat was a Vietnamese Private. He and his weapon faced the rear and flanks of the vehicle. In the front passenger seat, Sergeant Ling sat with a carbine. He was an interpreter for the district chief. The vehicle was driven by Captain Tinh. He was tall for an oriental. Some believed he had French blood in him. He wore glasses and carried two pistols, one on his hip in a holster and the other in his belt under his khaki shirt. He was demanding and cruel to all of his subordinates. To those above him he deferred to their judgment with reverence. In many aspects he had missed his calling as a feudal war lord. Captain Tinh was vain, conceited, and corruptible. He was also a creature of habit. He awoke every day at the same hour and always had the same breakfast in the same cafe. He always had lunch and a nap from twelve o'clock to two o'clock. Every Sunday he went to see his girl in Paris-ton Qui. And every night he remained until after dark in the refugee camp as of late. He could be located and killed any time and any place. The odds were not in his favor.

The jeep came to a screeching halt. Barbed wire was stretched across the road. A light flashed in their face. Acknowledgment of recognition was made. They had reached the first checkpoint on the road. The Koreans waived them on and removed the barrier from the road. The jeep moved slowly. Tinh flashed his headlights. Some one hundred meters down the road was a second barrier. It, too was removed so they could pass through.

The three men were off again and into the night.

Quiet murmuring voices could be heard along the route at various points if the jeep were to slow down. Peasants and merchants were enjoying their family supper. Dim lights flickered from earthen stoves. Fireflies flashed in the night air. And grandparents told stories to children about times past and dead heroes. Whiffs of incense filled the air...hovered near the ground and then rose into the atmosphere of the night. The wind was changing eastward to southeast and finally it came directly from the south. It would rain again tonight

The jeep stopped at a road junction. The occupants got out and entered a small cafe. They all ordered Chinese noodle soup, rice, a sweet roll, and a beer. This was Lum's. They stopped here often. The restaurant extended to the road itself. A roof covered the kitchen and sleeping quarters in the back. There were four roadside tables with small stools or benches on each side of the tables. Postcards and newspaper advertisements were nailed to the walls inside to serve as decorations. The calendar from USAID was three years old. But each month had a different and picturesque portrayal of aspects of Vietnamese life. A scrawny brown and white mongrel dog lay on the floor. It survived from day to day from the table scraps. In one corner there was a pile of sawdust. A child was standing over the sawdust and urinating on it. The men asked for ice in their beer. The owner walked to the corner of the room, pushed the sawdust aside, and chopped off some ice with his knife. He replaced the sawdust and brought the ice over to the table and placed it in their glasses. The cold beer and hot soup tasted good. No one was bothered by the ants on rolls or by dead mosquitoes in the soup. They finished the meal with a hot drink. The sergeant and the guard had tea. Captain Tinh had *café au lait*. He became disturbed because there was a chicken feather and a piece of eggshell in his cup. The owner came over and apologized and poured his coffee into another cup. They finished, paid the bill, and left.

Lum wiped the remaining food off the plates with a dirty rag and replaced the dishes on the shelf. He took the chop sticks and wiped them on his trouser leg one by one. He placed them back in the glass on the table for use. He tossed out the remaining ice and beer on the ground. His glasses were clean. The dog ate the ice and licked up the scraps of rice and noodles on the dirt floor.

As the jeep pulled away and left the cafe, a young boy and girl arrived on a Honda. They ordered dinner at Lum's.

The jeep with the three occupants in it darted down the lonely road. Somewhere ahead in the distance a group of men were waiting for them. The final outcome was determined before they ever reached that one particular instance and point in time. They would, if they were lucky, die in a quick manner without much pain. If captured another fate worse than death would befall them.

The jeep passed a row of fruit vendors on the road. Their wood stands stood along the side of the road. They offered oranges the size of grapefruit and as sweet as lemons. There was an ample supply of sugar cane. Mangos, bananas, and pineapple were cut into halves and offered for sale. The vendors were for the most part children and old women. They would curl up on the rickety tables at night and sleep surrounded by their produce. During the day they did a large business with passing civilian buses. As the jeep sped past them they were getting ready for bed and, in fact, some were already asleep or didn't care to notice the jeep. One old woman in particular wondered why the men in the sentry house on the bridge hadn't sent for fruit tonight to have with their dinner.

As the jeep veered around a corner it came

into sight of the bridge. It began to slow down because of the barbed wire obstacles placed on the road at night.

"Get ready; this may be them," Troung whispered. The vehicle passed their hiding place. Troung said nothing. He got into a kneeling position and opened fire with his weapon. His men began to fire also. The jeep started to speed up and crash through the barrier to reach the protection of the sentry house. The private in the rear seat fired one clip from his rifle and jammed in another one. Bullets hit the tires of the vehicle and slammed into the engine of the jeep. The windshield caved in as bullets smashed into it. The guard jumped from the jeep just as it gained entrance to the bridge carrying the barbed wire under and around the front tires of the jeep. At this point Roan signaled for the first mine to be fired. The private caught the entire blast as he jumped from the jeep. His body was blown into a thousand directions. Pieces of him landed back in the jeep. Tinh and the sergeant were soaked with blood.

The jeep wouldn't move any farther. Troung and his men were darting back and forth across the road behind them. Tinh and the sergeant were down on the ground returning fire in both directions. Roan touched off the other claymore mine on his end of the bridge. Both men were low enough to the ground that they escaped serious injury from the mine. Bleeding from glass cuts they still returned fire to the attackers.

Roan told Xuyen to rush them on the bridge. He rushed out the door firing his thompson as he went. He ran in a crouched position. The sergeant on the bridge cut him down with his carbine. He jerked to the side and hit the side of the bridge and rolled over the top of the rail into the water below.

Hinh triggered the explosive charge on the bridge itself. It went off with a tremendous roar. The entire center section of the bridge began to slide into the water, and wood and broken supports groaned as the bridge slipped away. More firing from Troung's men set the gas tank of the jeep on fire. It exploded with a deafening roar. A second explosion occurred as some small arms ammunition went up in the jeep. The bridge looked like the fourth of July.

With the center of the bridge gone, the jeep added too much weight to the side, on which it sat. Slowly the bridge began to tilt to one side. The jeep began to slide towards the water. The sergeant screamed as the entangled wire on the jeep caught his leg. He dropped his rifle and tried to free himself frantically. Tinh grabbed the rifle and fired again toward Troung and his men. They were the closest now and the most immediate threat. Another burst of bullets from the jungle found their mark. The sergeant moaned and stopped struggling. His arm was shot away. The jeep turned on its side, flipping the sergeant on top and the flames reached out to him and began to burn his clothes. He felt nothing as he was dead.

Then the jeep fell over the side of the bridge and into the water below. There was a loud splash and a hissing sound as the water extinguished the flames. An eerie light silhouetted the bridge now. Tinh was alone. The carbine was out of ammunition. He was trapped. There was no way out except the river. Tinh looked around him. He shoved a pistol in his pocket and began to crawl on his stomach towards the opening in the bridge.

Roan shouted to Troung to keep firing as he was getting away. Again the firing began with a vengeance. Tinh made it to the edge and dropped over the side. He fell into space and freedom in the night. Halfway down he struck a piling that had been exposed and broken into a jagged piece by the blast.

His body sank into the wood like a hot knife into butter. His head jerked back—his legs and arms struggled to free himself by reflex. His mouth opened to scream but no sound emerged except the gurgle of blood as it dripped from his open mouth. Troung stood on the bridge looking over him. He raised his rifle and fired into the body to make sure that the job was complete. The bullets chopped through the warm flesh of Tinh. His body seemed to dance on the pole as if held there by electricity. When the firing ceased is entire body fell limp. Tinh was dead.

Time has ceased for all those concerned. In what was just six minutes it felt like an eternity to some, and for a few of them it was eternity. But the clock of time moves inexorably forward, and these men had to leave now too.

Roan was thinking as he looked down upon the debris of the bridge and in the water. Within the knowledge and grasp of man there is only life. This he can understand until he confronts death, which lasts only for a brief instant until one is dead. Man cannot explain it, but he can create either life form himself. Life is something he has never really refined to make it something more infinitely beautiful than it is. Death he can make short or long and drawn out with pain and suffering. He has created weapons to kill none to make life. Strange that man in his intellectual and animal quest to better himself, cannot raise above his animal relatives, which have no reasoning power, no mind that can think and sort facts and make rational decisions. Instead man takes the simple solution, and that is to wipe out the opposition so that it may not threaten his existence and his way of thinking.

Philosophers and kings write books to make perfect societies. Their adherents…man…take these ideas and force them down the throats of others by the sword regardless of whether or not they want or desire to be enlightened.

Chapter Six
Nichols

It was five-thirty in the morning when specialist Hubble awoke Captain Nichols. "Sir, sir, you have to get up. We have got to fly a special mission. Sir, get up—it's Hubble."

"What's the trouble, John?" Nichols asked as he peered out at the darkness of his tent and hearing the voice of this close friend and companion. He blinked his eyes and finally the world began to come into focus. Suddenly he leaped up to a sitting position.

"Are we being attacked again?" he inquired with a note of urgency in his voice.

"No, sir. The VC killed the District Chief last night. We got a request to run a psy-war mission, asking members in the unit to give up and telling the people of their crimes. We are to take off at 0600. I put the speakers on the aircraft already. It is going to be a live broadcast on very short notice. Sergeant Tam is up and getting a script together."

"Thanks for letting me sleep a little. How about leaflets?" By this time, his shirt was on and he was pulling on his fatigues over his boots. Most everyone slept in their boots. One never knew when they would get mortared at night. In which case they had to run for a bunker.

"Well, sir, Sergeant Tagger is on duty as the TOC and he helped me load 50,000 safe conduct passes. I figure that should be enough to drop over the area. Tagger has the request from Division and can brief you on the area and the situation, sir."

By this time Nichols was dressed and putting on his helmet and web gear. He picked up his rifle that was resting against the side of his bed.. "Okay, I'm ready, let's go!"

The two men stepped outside. It was raining gently. There was ground fog in the air.

Their feet splashed through the mud as they made their way to the operations center. A dog barked and snarled in the dark. The lights in the mess hall were on. Cooks were busy in the kitchen getting the morning breakfast ready for the troops. They stepped in the kitchen entrance to grab a cup of coffee and hot roll.

"Another early mission, sir?"

"Roger—one day is like the rest—never a dull moment. Send out the boys with some coffee for the pilots, will you, Red?"

"It's done already, sir. Don't fly too low, sir. Charlie would love that captain!"

"You know me, Red. I would never think of doing such a thing."

"That's why I mentioned it, sir. Word gets around about all the chances you guys take. I understand the pilots don't like flying your missions. Is that right, sir?"

"Well, I can think of a lot of things and places I would rather be too, Red. But It's only for a year, you know. Anyone can take it for a year. Hell, my father spent four years in the Pacific. So I guess I can put up with one year here. Thanks for the coffee, as usual. See you at lunch!"

"Yes, sir. See you at lunch." The old sergeant turned away and went back to scrambling eggs and cooking SOS as usual.

They both skirted around the sandbag bunker that was next to the mess hall. It was big enough to accommodate thirty men. More than once they had all been in there, Nichols thought to himself. The operations center was about sixty meters away. On the other side of it was a chopper pad. A Robinhood ship was there, they noticed, it's blades idling in the first rays of morning twilight. Except for them and sergeant Tagger, the office was empty. As they came in the sergeant was sitting by the radios and passing the time away reading a cheesecake novel with some blond stretched out on a bed on the cover of the book. He put the book down when he saw the captain.

"Good morning, sir."

"Hi, sarge. Well…give us the low down for this one. Just what is so important to drag us out of bed at this hour of the morning?"

"Captain Tinh, the District Chief that was working at the refugee center, got murdered on his way home last night. From what we can piece together there were two or three others with him at the time. They got hit on route one on that one-lane bridge. His body was left dangling on a wooden spike. He was shot up real bad, and there was blood all over the remaining part of the bridge. Sector called Division and wants us to tell the populace about the ambush and VC atrocities. Just the same story, sir. Maybe you can just change the message some. Anyway they also requested that we broadcast a message to B-40 and C-402. G-2 figures that it was probably one of these units that made the hit last night. Intelligence places them still in the An Loi area. At least that is what they have received from agent reports operating in the vicinity. So in essence, you are to fly route one along the river between the refugee camp and An Loi and some of the surrounding areas and drop leaflets and play your messages. You have the ship for two hours. That's about it, sir."

"Okay, thanks, sergeant. Hubble—plot our map so we can point the areas out to the pilots. Where is Sergeant Tam?"

"I'm here, sir." Tam appeared in the doorway, He was short and thin. His black hair was slick and greasy on his head. When he smiled you noticed that all of his front teeth were gold. It assured him that he would have a proper and expensive burial. Tam had a sister studying in the United States. She was always sending him socks and canned foods from the States. Tam had been a lawyer in civilian life. He refused a commission because it meant eight years in the service. At least as an enlisted sergeant-interpreter he had only six years to do. He seemed to enjoy his work, but he would always disappear on the weekends. For him the war was only five days a week. And because he did such a good job, no one ever mentioned his regular absences to see his family. Tam was, in short, a good soldier. He had only one bad mark on his record. He had fought with the French and had been an officer. He had deserted them and returned to civilian life. "I have recorded a message on the tape, sir. But I only had a chance to make it once. Would you like me to translate it for you?"

"Fine, sergeant, go ahead."

"Attention, attention; the Viet Cong have committed another murder in the name of liberty and justice. Last night they killed your district chief, the man who helped all of you with your fight against the criminal communists. If you know where these murderers are hiding, tell your local police, and then we shall deal the death blow against them. Members of B-40 and C-402...give yourselves up and rally to the just cause of the government. You will be treated fairly. We will take care of you and your families. Surrender before your leaders lead you to an unmarked grave and dishonorable death. Rally to the government now before it is too late. Attention, attention...what do you think of that, sir?"

"Normally I think that it would be better to use two separate messages for a better effect.

However, with the shortage of time, this should prove to be fine. Just add that they can take one of the leaflets and turn themselves in with it because it is a safe-conduct pass."

"Yes, captain, I will add it at the end of the message."

"Sergeant Tagger, notify the ship that we are on our way and to crank it up."

"Roger…Robin Hood thirty-eight, this is Raider Zulu, Raider four-two Charlie and party are on the way—over."

"This is Robin Hood thirty-eight —Wilco out."

And so with rifles, maps, tape recorders, and tape and flack jackets dangling from their hands, the three men headed towards the aircraft. Once in the aircraft, they began throwing their equipment inside. As the blades turned faster, the whine of the engines grew louder and the grass and dirt around the helicopter began to wave from the blasts of air until dust and debris were thrown all over. Hubble was putting on his flack jacket while Nichols was briefing the pilots on the mission. With that finished, Nichols placed his flack jacket on his seat as did Tam. Both men were married and it was a matter of personal priority as to where one puts his jacket. Most pilots prefer to save the family jewels. Nichols always wondered if the expression "to ride by the seat of your pants" was a chopper pilot expression. In any case, he always figured that at great heights, a bullet would enter from the bottom of the craft; besides the side doors were always open so that both gunners could have a clear field of vision to fire. Nichols noticed that the ground fog was beginning to clear. They should have a clear morning for the flight.

The tail of the ship rose up and the front was down like a charging bull. They hovered for a moment and suddenly they lifted off the pad in a roar of engines. Most of the pilots wanted to gain as much height as possible before they left the air space over the base. Thus they reverted to a power take off. The loud speakers were a lot of extra weight, not to mention the leaflets. With the speakers hanging over the side of one door they made a beautiful target for the VC. For some reason they had a special delight on shooting at psy-war ships. And because of the speakers they were easily identified.

Below them was the base camp. Tents, bunkers, showers, latrines, mess halls, tin buildings, barbed wire, trucks, tanks, jeeps, artillery positions, paths that were dirt roads, and items and all sorts of instruments of war were stretched below them. Soon they were over the vast complex. The morning sun had begun to cast shadows on the land below. Straw hats and buffalo were moving into the fields. The rice paddies reflected the sun's rays like small jewels in the landscape. Most of the paddies were square or rectangle shape. They were separated by small dikes, and the entire scene stretched for miles as far as the eye could see. It was broken by occasional jungle areas and small villages meeting at the crossroads of dirt paths that were the communication link of the country. Scooters, bikes, and people were beginning to fill the roads with traffic. Smoke from cooking fires filtered into the morning air from the villages. Elsewhere smoke was being filtered off into lean-tos in jungle areas of the Viet Cong. The world was awakening and moving on in its moment of time and space. The roar of the engines and the swish of the winds prevailed in the plane. The only way to communicate was through the intercom in the plane. It was cool and lonely in this place in the sky. Below then another helicopter flew past them heading north by northwest toward the Michelin rubber plantation. Above them three Vietnamese Sky Raiders swept past in "V" formation flying towards some unknown target to them. The pilot speaking to base artillery operation to avoid flying over strike zones in the early morning. Once in a while a pilot would forget to ask and he suddenly found himself in the middle of falling shells. The only evasive action was to hit the deck which was dangerous in open rice fields but not as much over jungle areas.

They were now over the refugee camp. Hubble turned on the speakers and the message began. The plane flew over the area for fifteen minutes and gradually flew wider circles to cover more territory. Finally they left the area of the camp and headed in the direction of the ambush site. After a few minutes, they could see the destroyed bridge below them. People were already beginning to work on its repair. In the water they could see the form of a jeep. They circled here for a few minutes and then headed for An Loi and the jungle area around it. Somewhere down there within hearing and even shooting distance of their plane were the men who had done the killing. Perhaps the message would reach one of them, Nichols thought to himself. He preferred this job than to be on the ground slugging it out with the enemy. This was more impersonal and had intellectual challenge. He had to deal with the brain of the enemy. He had to match his cunning and propaganda with their own. Just three weeks ago, he had gotten an immediate response from his messages. An entire six-man squad had defected with their weapons to the government. It was successes like this that justified his job in the war. He was bringing peace without bloodshed. This was certainly much better than the other way. Friendly persuasion was the only answer in this whole mess in which both sides found themselves at the present time. We couldn't extract our troops from the war without losing alliances in Asia. And the communists couldn't stop without admitting defeat. So far it was a stalemate and he knew it. All of those exaggerated reports of pacification progress and tremendous victories were solely for home consumption. The entire thing was balancing on a razor's edge and it could go either way. Since the communists wouldn't talk peace the only way was to make their men listen to ideas of peace and coming home and to turn the population against them.

Hubble was tapping him on the shoulder. He was motioning towards the ear set. He had a message on the radio. Nichols struggled with the ear set, getting it over his helmet.

"Raider four-two Charlie—this is Raider Zulu—over."

"Raider four-two Charlie—over."

"Zulu. Raider six needs a ship for recon mission...break...have you nearly finished the mission...break... if so return to base operations and Zulu station...over."

"Roger...this is four-two Charlie...have completed mission on first time around and will return to Zulu out."

Nichols gave Hubble the earphones and got out of his seat to talk with the pilots. He tapped one on the shoulder and began shouting in his ear to return to Zulu. The pilot acknowledged, and with a wide arc the ship began heading back to the camp. Nichols made a waving motion with this hand to indicate to sergeant Tam that they were returning to camp. Tam smiled as flying usually made him sick anyway.

Today, and for all those concerned, this had been a routine mission. They did, however, have 20,000 leaflets left when they had received the call to return to the base. Over the An Loi jungle Tam dumped the whole bunch of them. From the ground, it looked like the ticker tape parades in New York City. Nichols knew that the leaflets had many uses to the people. They served as toilet paper, cigarette paper, fuel for lighting small fires and, once in a great while, someone actually used one for its intended purpose…as a safe conduct pass. So, in some small measure they all played, the three of them, a small role in the overall effort of pacification of the countryside.

The flight back to base was direct and much shorter than the flight out that morning. Waiting for them on the pad was Major Lancaster. As the ship landed he jumped aboard and signaled for the pilots to take off again. He sat on the end seat and strapped himself in with the safety belt. He put on the ear phones.

"Robin Hood thirty-eight—this is Raider six. Head towards x-ray Tango 749-831. Do you roger—over?"

"Thirty-eight Wilco—out."

At the top of his voice he shouted to Nichols that a convoy was being ambushed and they were to fly air cover as this was the most available ship in the area.

Nichols in turn just shouted they were going after Victor Charlie's up north of the camp. He then fought the wind wiping through the ship and pointed out the area on the map to his two men.

The speakers on the side of the ship prevented it from reaching maximum speed because of weight and wind resistance. The chopper was making some one hundred knots, and at this rate it took them fifteen minutes to reach the area. Below them a truck was in flames. It had been the lead truck, and all the other vehicles were prevented from getting around it. Men in other trucks were lying in the road bed and returning fire in both directions. The entire perspective was not dissimilar to playing war with tiny tin soldiers in a sandbox.

With a noise like tremendous static on the radio, the door gunners opened up on VC positions on both sides of the road. All men felt the empty feeling and tingling sensation of the top of a roller-coaster as the shipped dived for a low-level strafing run. Lancaster had his M-16 in his lap; he raised it and began to fire into the jungle. Empty casings fell on the floor of the ship and rolled out when it tilted back for another run at the position. The co-pilots were calling in artillery on their position. So they had time for one more sweep over the area. Nichols was on the right side of the ship with the speakers. He felt a strange excitement. One is so detached from the situation. He slammed a cartridge into his weapon and he too became involved with the men on the ground. As he raised his rifle, two men broke from a bush to his right rear. He fired—the tracers seemed to cut the area apart. The gunner was firing at the same target. One of the VC fell forward and bounced twice before he stopped moving. The other either dived into another series of bushes or he too was hit but Nichols could not tell. There was a loud twang and metal flew through the entire cockpit of the chopper. A slug had hit the loud speakers.

Hubble was lying on the floor and his lips were moving. He was saying something but no one could hear. Blood was running down his shoulder and arm. Part of his right ear was gone. Nichols was the first to see him there. He took one look and threw up on the floor of the ship. He grabbed a flack jacket from the seat and placed it under Hubble's feet. He took his canteen and fed him some water. Lancaster was still firing and Tam untied a first aid kit from behind the pilots seat. He took out a needle and then inserted it in Hubble's arm. Nichols took a knife and ripped off his shirt. Blood was oozing from the wounds. At least it wasn't an artery, he thought to himself. He took his hand and wiped his mouth as he was still drooling vomit.

By this time Lancaster had noticed what had happened. He told the pilot to hover near the center of the convoy to pick up as many wounded as they could get aboard. He then switched to the frequency of the convoy.

"Hauler three, this is raider six—over."

"Ah raider six, this is hauler three—over."

"Six, we are coming down for one minute—we have one wia on board—we can take five or six of your people if you can get them to us...over."

"Three wilco and thanks...break—what about artillery—over?"

"Six—it is on the way...break...you should have another ship in your location in zero four—over."

"Three—roger; I am throwing smoke—do

you identify—over?"

"Six, ah roger, ah roger—I identify green smoke…green, smoke—over."

"Three affirmative—out."

The pilot did an auto rotation in coming into the landing zone, which is to say that he dropped straight down like a rock using his blades as a parachute. The gunners continued to fire until they were only ten feet off the ground. The ship hovered in the air about one foot off the ground. The pilot would not touch down because they were afraid of landing on a mine meant for a vehicle. A lieutenant came rushing up with four litter bearers behind him.

"Thanks a million, sir. Take care of my boys—they are hurt pretty bad…" Nichols could not hear any more of the conversation because of the noise of the chopper and the firing on the ground which was distinct and more clear now. His gunner on the speaker side was opening up with his machine gun again. Tracers were streaking in an arc into a wooded knoll about one hundred meters away form their position. Nichols followed the direction of the gunner and began firing with his weapon too. Tam was beside him and also firing. They had just got the last man aboard when a mortar round hit the earth some thirty meters to their left. Dirt, dust, and metal were flying into the air. Before the dirt could settle on the ground, the ship gave a lurch and was airborne once again. The lieutenant was diving for the ground. Where the ship had been two more mortar rounds hit with extreme accuracy. Every gun on the chopper was blazing away at the jungle below in hopes of finding a shadowy target.

The chopper had gained enough altitude so that the mortars were not effective. Almost simultaneously artillery began coming in on the VC positions. This forced the crew to low level at some ninety knots at tree-top level. The ship hopped over roofs, hedges, and trees heading south. It remained right above route thirteen and twisted and turned with the road. At this height and speed, if the chopper crashed, there would be no survivors.

Lancaster glanced at Nichols and the wounded men. For one slight second there seemed to be a haunted look in his eyes. He cupped his hands over the mike and began speaking.

"Raider zulu, raider six."

"Raider zulu, raider six."

"Raider zulu, raider six," he said not giving the other station a chance to break in on the circuit. His voice raised in anger each time he spoke.

Six, zulu...go."

"This is six. What took you so long?...break...I have several wia with me. Have the first med get an ambulance to the pad...break...call the control tower on lima and find out where the FAC is. These people still need help...break...when I return I want the name and grade of the operator on duty as Zulu station...break...call playboy switch and get in touch with playboy six. Tell him the coordinates of the ambush and have him send a reaction force. Do you roger this transmission over?"

"Six, zulu—roger."

"Six out!"

There was one sure thing about this war, Nichols thought, and that was that you can depend on the medics. They were on the pad as the ship touched down. They had plasma, blankets, stretchers, and bandages for whatever the occasion might warrant. They were aboard the craft before it had touched the ground and settled. There wouldn't be room on the ambulance, so Nichols went back to the office to find a jeep and go over to the hospital to find out the condition of Hubble.

Sergeant Perez was the duty NCO on the radio. He looked rather pale when the major entered. It was he who had been on the horn when the major had called in for help. Before either man could say anything, Captain Luttner intervened in the situation. He was he new S-2 and Sergeant Perez usually worked in his shop except this particular day when he had to pull the duty

"Sir, I monitored the conversation and I just want to say, sir, that Sergeant Perez is a fine NCO. However he has, as you know, an intelligence MOS, which means, sir, that he, like many of the men, lack experience on the radio. You will note, sir, that all of your instructions were carried out to the letter."

"All right, captain, we will let it go this time. But seeing that you know so much about radio procedure, it will be your responsibility to see that every man in this outfit is briefed and thoroughly familiar with radio procedures. Now is that clear, captain?"

"Yes, sir, I will see to it right away."

The face of Sergeant Perez was enough to thank Captain Luttner. There was relief and gratitude in it. Like most Latin faces, emotion, worry, love, and hate could be realized by viewing the face and not waiting to hear the word.

"Hey, Jack—how about giving me a run down on the way things stand on the situation map. Then I can brief the pilots on the latest intelligence."

"Sure, Doug—come on over to my section. Now as you see here we have had a lot of small-type incidents in the last forty-eight hours. The VC are operating in small-type units generally. But I would make the conjecture that they are covering up the movement of large units coming out of war zone 'D'."

We have had no current agent reports on these larger groups for at least two weeks. By observing the map, all the incidents are occurring south of us or just in our general area. Now if we divert troops to cover these areas here, then we leave a large gap in our defenses in the north. I think there VC are moving men and supplies into the Iron Triangle and getting ready for a monsoon offensive. Off hand I would suggest that no one fly this area without two gunships to go with you. I have made out a target list for artillery that would bracket these four main villages at night and also cover these two smaller hamlets. I think the communists are resting up here. And I think the guerillas in our area are taking their orders from here. An Loi, south of us, is probably still the base of operations for the guerillas. But again this is only the small units. I have told division that we can expect a large attack on our base within a week's time or they will skirt us on the river and head for Saigon."

"Do you really think it is that serious, Jack?"

"Nichols...this is my second tour, and nothing—and I mean nothing—would surprise me. Look between us and the Iron Triangle—there are only four South Vietnamese outposts. And they are so far apart that they are worthless and could in any event be over run easily by a determined force if necessary. And to boot, you know and I know that the pacification for all that it is worth on paper is just that...on paper. The people on the whole are simply not responding in great droves and numbers to the government. My God, you can't blame them. We don't have the men to act as the watch dog for the entire countryside. If the South Vietnamese wouldn't help themselves...then who is going to do it. Lord, we are fighting their battles for them already. Yet they still will not commit themselves either for their country or their people."

"Jack, you just can't believe what you just told me. What about the defector program? Just last week we got an entire squad to defect to our side. Now I think that is progress. Sure it may be slow and a long road for a final outcome…but, at least we are getting some type of response."

"Doug, what evidence do you have that they just surrendered—not because of new-found loyalty but because they were afraid to die at this point in time. Or that perhaps it was their mission to defect and then to infiltrate the program and kill the district chief or some other government official. Sure they provide information. Some of that is of great military value…yesterday. Not today. Granted perhaps a few are sincere. But I wouldn't trust the entire program."

"Listen—you are wrong." Nichols was now getting excited and was speaking faster. "I have been down to the Center for these people on many occasions and have used them for propaganda missions. And on the whole they are sincere. They have stood there and asked their friends to defect and leave the VC. They have told them that they have been well treated. We have sent their families to them…"

"How do you know that these friends, as you call them, are not in reality government supporters or people they have some grudge against. You give them a chance. Christ, when you call out those names over an area and tell them that you know that they want to defect and now is their chance..shit, the VC would drop them on the spot."

"But, Jack, that is part of the point. If they are VC, and they don't want to defect, they will almost be forced into it because we cast

97

doubt into their ranks about one another. Either way we win…can't you see that?"

"Sure I see it…but that still is not winning the hearts and minds of the people. We are not getting to them. Don't forget the Japanese, Chinese, and French all thought that they were winning too. I have noticed that they are all gone or have mixed ethnically with the people. The same thing can happen to us and the people know it. We may stay here for five years or even twenty years, but in the end we will have to leave. There will be other places we have to defend. There will be other political priorities."

"Well I guess we are agreeing only from different angles. But of course no one knows back home about the losses we are taking in Cambodia, Laos, and Korea right now. I understand that they all figure on the Vietnam casualties. Listen let's go have a beer and some lunch. Besides, I have to get over to the hospital and see Hubble."

"Great. What happened out there anyway?"

"Well, we were just on our second run over the area…"

The two men walked out of the office and towards the mess hall. Harper entered from the opposite door and sat down at his desk. He was getting ready to take a convoy into Saigon to pick up supplies for the refugees.

Chapter Seven

Saigon

The afternoon was hot and muggy. A man's body would stick to his clothes and the clothes stick to the seats of jeeps, chairs, or anything else. The sun would heat metal so hot you couldn't touch it without burning yourself. Inside the office the overhead fans were circulating hot air. Major Lancaster had left on the chopper again with Noble, his driver and radio operator.

Harper was scrutinizing the map on his desk. He was engrossed in the routes to Saigon. One hand was supporting his head while the other was tracing out routes from the camp to Saigon.

Benjeman entered the office. He was wearing a flack jacket over his civilian clothes; it was unbuttoned. There was a butt of a .38 special banging out from a shoulder holster.

"The trucks are here and ready to go."

"Is that the noise I heard...let's take a look."

They walked outside the office; ten vintage trucks were standing there. Four were

Japanese army trucks which looked as if they would never make it. The others were various 1920 Ford models. All looked absolutely terrible. There was a guard with each driver.

"My God, Benjeman, they will never make it on a round trip. Where in the world did you find this stuff?"

"I have got a contractor who owes me a debt. This fleet carries garbage off your base when they aren't working for me."

"That's just great. I won't be part of such an operation."

"Lancaster says you will! Remember? Now stop farting around and get the MP gun jeep out here and let's go. We have got people waiting for us in Saigon." Benjeman smiled and added: "Look, I will make it worth your while. I'll fix you up with a steam bath at the Caravelle Hotel. The trucks will take all night to load up so we can enjoy the town. We can make some stops on Thu Duc Street and hit the bars and the broads. Listen, it will be a real break from the routine here. You are going to enjoy it."

"Yeah, sure, sure, that's fine. But this convoy is going to give me an ulcer both ways…and that's if we make it both ways." And then he added almost inaudibly…" Besides, the fact that I think you are crooked from the word go and that you couldn't operate the way you do unless your actions were condoned in Saigon."

"What did you say, Harper?"

"Nothing."

"Sorry, thought you said something to me."

Harper picked up the field phone on his desk and began to crank it to get the operator.

"Hello...hello...hello switch...SWITCH right, this is main 42...give me mike papa six romeo...hello switch—did...Sarge, is that you...good, listen, we are ready for your people...we are ready for your people. They will be here in five minutes—good...thanks—out!"

The two men went out into the heat of the day to meet the escort jeep. There was one driver and a sergeant on the mounted machine gun in the back of the jeep. The jeep itself was a small arsenal. Harper got in the front seat to act as guide and Benjeman got into the back seat and sat on one wheel fender behind the driver. The sergeant stood up and balanced himself on the machine gun. There was no windshield and in its place there was a row of sandbags encased in ammunition boxes which were tied down to the hood of the engine. Both the military policemen wore goggles. Harper ran back into the office and took his and fastened them over his helmet and got a pair of sun glasses for Benjeman.

They began to slowly move out. Harper explained to the driver that they would follow route thirteen until the Bein Hoa cut off and take it until they could link up with route one. Then they would head west and into the Saigon-Gia Dinh area and there they would find Le Cong Street and could then proceed south to the dock area and the logistical command.

"If we get hit on the way in, don't wait for stragglers, just keep going and don't stop for anything. We are the only Americans in this convoy, and I want us to return tomorrow in the same manner in which we left…in one piece."

Already the dust from the road was seeping into everything—clothes, weapons everything that it could find was covered with the powdered clay and sand. Men came back from the roads looking like coal workers who had been in the mines for weeks without a bath. Only the rain would bring respite.

After a few minutes, they reached the main gate. There were cement bunkers on each side of the entrance. The entire area was covered with barbed wire and sentries. They stopped every vehicle and asked for convoy papers and inquired as to the destination and time of return of the men. Because they were riding in the MP jeep they stopped and told them that the ten trucks belonged to them for a convoy to Saigon. The MP's knew each other and chatted for a moment and joked about the convoy. They were then waved through the gates. Once through the gates they were in the open country. The first village was two miles down the road. Between the village and the base camp, there was a Vietnamese headquarters of armor and mechanized infantry. This group had taken part in the overthrow of the Diem regime several years before. Politically they were not reliable. Militarily they were a formidable force and good fighters when they had the proper leadership.

The dirt road was filled with civilian and military traffic. The road itself was gutted from the rains and the traffic and no one bothered to fix it. At points it was single-lane traffic, and the largest vehicle had the right of way. Thus large US convoys rolled through the countryside unhindered. Once in awhile, they were stopped because of an accident when a truck would run over a lambretta and the driver. Then they had to wait to make a report to the national police and pay the individual for the vehicle. If he still was living after running into a two and one-half ton truck. On this day, villagers were going to market in their ox carts. The old carts swayed back and forth on the road and straining from the weight of wood, rice, fruit, cement, tobacco, pigs, chickens, or whatever the cargo might be, including weapons for the Viet Cong. But it was impossible to search every one.

After about twenty minutes the convoy reached the outskirts of Phu Goung, the Province capital. It was a beautiful old French city. There were brick streets and towering buildings with wide variands and circular driveways. The market was down next to the river. The Province house sits on a hill overlooking the entire city. Close by to the north is the old French fort that is now used for a Vietnamese engineer school. It too has a view of the city and sits on the edge of the river. Leading up to its gates are the once proud French estates of governors and high officials now laying in ruin and inhabited by peasants that have left the countryside to prosper in the city only to find worse poverty and misery. Forty families live in one house. Children are everywhere. The beauty of the landscape is tarnished by the smell of poverty, disease, decay, and destitution. The convoy slowed down by the bus station because of the heavy traffic. Soon they were past it, and on the left was the national police station and across the street was the headquarters for civilian intelligence. There were Chinese guards all over the area. No one could stop in front of either entrance. Just a few minutes past this spot they were once again in the country. Soon the road twisted into the rolling hills. Generally it followed the Saigon River here and there. They passed bridge after bridge with the small sentry house and guard contingent. The soldiers were laying in hammocks along the bridges with their rifles across their laps or they were swimming in the river while one man held the weapons on the bridge. Some were sitting there smoking or talking to one of the local girls and waving to the traffic as it went by.

After one hour they reached route one at the Bien Hoa cutoff. It was the largest highway in South Vietnam. It was four lanes of traffic at this point going in both directions.

One of the drivers behind the jeep was honking his horn. His engine was overheated and he couldn't go any further. Harper had the convoy keep moving. If the man wanted his money he knew where to go in the city. He could catch up later in the day if possible or take his chances on the road at night. The man was shaking his fists at the convoy, but no one paid attention. They kept on moving. His guard jumped off the vehicle and caught the last truck in the convoy. He did not want to be left behind, even on this road.

Finally in the distance was the last bridge into Saigon, the Capital itself. Traffic was stop and go. The streets were teeming with millions of people. Bikes, scooters, trucks, cars, carts, jeeps, and pedestrians clogged the roads. The smell of fish, meat, humans, decay, paint, gas, and oil were all mixed together to form the smell of the Capital. In the rivers and canals of the city, people were drinking, washing, and defecating in the same water only feet apart.

Beggars and merchants, soldiers and policemen, mothers and whores, entertainers and criminals all mixed elbow to elbow on the streets and sidewalks. The black market was omnipresent. For a price anything could be bought—guns, cameras, food, cigarettes, jeeps, soap, leather goods…young boys or young girls, according to the taste of the buyer.

Most buildings had the look of a city besieged. Some still carried pockmarks of bullets from the French era. Cement was cracked and chipping on walls, posts, and buildings. Whitewashed brick was gray now with streaks of black, yellow, and brown. Vines and mold grew on walls unchecked. National monuments were covered with bird droppings and left in that condition for years. Thus original features, faces, and inscriptions could not be read or recognized. Mixing in the nameless crowds were westerners. They wore civilian clothing. They came from Germany, England, Poland, Italy, France, America, Canada, and Australia, and they arrived to work as agents, reporters, doctors, technicians, and more agents. Most stood above the crowd. They were easily recognized. They brought money, expense accounts, cars, women, bands, guns, corruption, influence, intrigue, and advice. For the most part they never left this city. Some did, but most remained. They wormed their way to the seats of power, invaders in an already ravaged country.

After traffic jams and more traffic jams, the convoy reached Gong Le Avenue. They headed south towards the docks and the world's biggest and busiest port. Along the way, they passed the Presidential Palace. It is a bold gothic structure, surrounded by soldiers, wire, bunkers, checkpoints, and police. Finally they reached the waterfront,. Resting in birth was a German hospital ship. They went over a canal and looked down on the decks of the ship.

As they crossed the bridge, the logistics command loomed up on their left. Blocks and blocks of warehouses, trucks, and row after row of ships on the wharves. They entered gate four and headed for the lumberyard.

"Hey, hold it up! What are you doing with all of these trucks in here?" A stern-faced colonel ran up to them.

"Sir, we are here to pick up materials for

the refugees in our area."

Benjeman jumped down from the jeep. "Colonel, my name is Benjeman", he said, extending his hand. "I am the USAID advisor up north of here. I have all the paperwork right here." He lifted a sheet of paper out of his pocket. It granted the authorization for the materials.

The Colonel took the papers and began reading. "It says here that you will bring in only five trucks. What are the rest doing here?"

"That is correct, colonel. As soon as we get these first five situated, I am taking the rest to a different location. I didn't want to create a traffic jam on the street. We will be out of here in a few minutes."

"Next time bring in only what you are authorized to bring in ..is that clear?"

"Yes, sir, and thanks a lot." Benjeman got back into the jeep.

As they left, the colonel was chewing out the MP at the main gate for not stopping the group and checking them out. As they turned a corner he was still shaking his fist in the face of the MP.

Stacks of lumber of all sizes and raising twenty feet into the air were all around them. A sergeant walked over from a small tin building and inquired if he could be of assistance. They explained that they needed to fill five trucks with lumber. He told them to roll them in an let the men start working. Harper released the gun jeep and told them to meet them at the same place at 11:00 the next morning.

With smiles and happiness, they turned the jeep around and headed towards the Brinks Hotel for fun and games. Harper and Benjeman got aboard the sixth truck. Benjeman explained they were going farther down the dock area. With hand motions, English, and a few words of Vietnamese, one understood the other. Harper was not sure which had understood. They drove along the wharves for about a mile. They reached a quartermaster depot. This time they were stopped by the gate guards. After they proved their identity, they were admitted to the grounds.

"Wait here! I am going to find Frank Corte." Benjeman disappeared behind a pile of boxes and equipment. They were sitting in the sun. The sweat streamed down their faces and soaked into their clothes. A few feet away, a woman was operating a hydraulic lift machine, and innovation which the war had brought to the country. Fatherless families needed a provider.

"I still don't understand how you did it, Benjeman." Harper lifted up his glass of beer and took another cool sip. "Come on how was the guy obligated to you? Christ, you are picking up military equipment."

"Listen—whenever a shipment comes in there is usually damaged goods that can be destroyed. So I just tell him what I want, and he sees that it goes on the expendable list. That is how we do it. And there is no one to get the wiser because before it can be checked out, I pick up the stuff. Now stop worrying about it, he will have all the correct paperwork in case we get stopped by the MP's or anyone else for that matter. It is almost the same thing as a combat loss. You write things off, and nobody cares one way or the other, as long as they have paperwork to back it up."

The band began to play "Long Tall Texan," and a young girl got on the stage and began to sing. Their waitress came over and asked if they would like another drink. She put her cool hands on the back of Harper's neck. Just the touch of a woman sent a chill up his spine. She whispered in his ear, "I love you, lieutenant, you buy me Saigon tea?" Without waiting for an answer, she sat on his lap. Her hands went inside his shirt and began to slowly scratch his chest. She put her head on his neck and curled up like a kitten. "You buy Sue Saigon tea?"

"Benjeman, what am I going to do with her?"

"If you like her, buy the tea and find out what she wants for a lay. There are plenty more where she came from."

"Okay, Sue, I buy you tea, but you bring over one number one friend for the man sitting with me."

The girl threw her legs into the air revealing her red pants underneath and landed on the floor. She half walked and half ran into a corner of the bar to find one of her friends to bring over the table. Shortly she returned with a lovely girl with gold capped teeth and hairy armpits. This cutie placed herself in

Benjeman's lap and began to nibble on his ear. Benjeman shifted his weight and pulled his pants down an inch—it was obvious that he was getting a hard on and was enjoying it.

In a few moments a waiter arrived at the table with two small shot glasses of darkly colored tea. He asked for 300 piasters and inquired if the men would like another drink.

"Hell, yes, bring us another drink." Harper downed his beer and then he asked the waiter to bring whiskey too. "Listen, Ben, why don't we get these broads crooked on boiler-makers. Then we can have it all night for nothing except for the cost of the booze and maybe a dinner over in the Chinese district. I have heard about the area and can't wait to get my teeth into some of their chow and even a broad if these two become a drag. How about it? What do you say—are you with me or not?"

"Sure, let's go, but we would have to get the permission of the owner to take his girls out of here until after closing hours. So let's go to the Rex Hotel and perhaps find some round eyes from Germany or France. Have a drink in the penthouse there. You have an entire view of the city and you can watch the war raging in the countryside from there. And then we can go to Cholon if you want or shack up with anything we find there. How does that sound?"

"Man, let's get to it. Drink up and let's go. First, I want to see if this girl has one or not." With that he ran his hand up her leg until he found her soft pants. He caught some hair and pulled it gently. Then he slipped his hand inside her pants and began to rub gently. She looked at him and smiled and asked if he would buy another tea. Harper said no. Her smile stopped—she jumped off his lap, and called him "Number ten fucking GI." She said a few other things and then sat in someone else's lap at the table next to theirs. "These people just don't believe in free love, do they, Ben?"

"You must be shitting me. Drink up and let's go. The day is still young." They both finished their drinks. And they walked outside into the heat of the day and the bright sunlight. The street was streaming with people going in all directions. The black marketeers covered every available space on the sidewalks. The two men grabbed a small blue and yellow taxi and left in the direction of the Rex Hotel. The view from the small cab was like a midget's view of the world. Everything was out of perspective. They were dwarfed by everything except the people on foot. They stopped for a light and everyone inched forward for a better position to get across the green light first. A motor bike scraped against the door. The driver yelled at the man and he ignored them.

They passed the Continental Hotel first with its outdoor restaurant. Harper could not understand why anyone would want to eat outside in this city. Dust and dirt was everywhere, not to mention the beggars and dogs which would approach an individual and hold out a dirty hand and beg for scraps of food from the table. Dogs would get inside and quarrel under your feet for food. No, that was not for him. Besides the Viet Cong had on numerous occasions thrown grenades or planted bombs in the sidewalk cafes for years. But it was humans nature not to learn from lessons of the past. Every new plane brought new fools into the country without the proper briefing on what to expect and without any knowledge about the face of the enemy or his tactics. Everything was in a world of gray until blood covered the land and sidewalks from the ignorance of the allied savior. Then every section would pass rules and regulations to meet the occasion of the moment. These people would leave and more would replace them, forgetting the rules of the past and indeed not even bothering to read them. Every day there was a turnover of hundreds of men going both ways. They were faces in the crowd, and numbers of faraway capitals and degrees of temperature lying in hospital beds from wounds and disease and stupidity

The Hotel Rex was the largest allied officer's club and hotel in Vietnam. It was surrounded with large pillars of solid concrete, put there to prevent a car with a bomb from crashing through the security around the hotel. Next to the building the visitor had to pass through paths of barbed wire and security guards. Once inside he checked in with Marine guards. At this point, all weapons were taken away and placed in safekeeping. No oriental was allowed beyond this point without a proper pass and few could even get this far unless they were part of the work force in the building. This building also housed allied government civilian offices for propaganda and other intelligence work.

The two men stepped inside an elevator and took the express car to the roof and the center of fun for visitors to Saigon. The penthouse was enclosed only with a roof. There were side bamboo curtains that could be dropped in bad weather. It seemed to be one of the tallest buildings in the capital city. There was a band which played continuously all day long and into the hours of the night.

Benjeman explained, "The dress is casual or come as you are. If you want to eat in the enclosed dining room, you must wear more appropriate clothing. There are fifty bar girls waiting to please the visitor, and there is ample bedroom space downstairs. This is the favorite watering spot of high ranking officers and civilians in the Capital. You will notice that it is not exclusively for them however." Benjeman continued to explain the area to Harper. Harper noticed a shapely blonde sitting at the bar. He excused himself for a moment and strode over to where she was sitting.

"Hi, lieutenant, my name is Dorothy Goddard—and what is yours?"

"Paul Harper. Just what are you doing here? I mean what are you doing in this country. You have some government position in the embassy or something?"

"No, Paul. I am here with the Red Cross to entertain the troops though I admit I never get outside of Saigon. We do have girls out in the sticks and more coming every day—perhaps there will be some where you are stationed before long. How far are you from here? You have the combat look which the fat asses here don't have."

"Yeah, well, we are far enough away to make it a lifetime. I am with the Division just north of here about thirty miles. You are going to be here for long...up here at the bar, I mean?"

"Perhaps."

"Listen, why don't you join me at my table and perhaps if your not busy you could have dinner with me. What do you say to that?"

"That sounds very nice. I noticed you had a friend with you when you came in. Joyce, the girl I came over with, is in the girl's room. Would it be all right if she would join us too?"

"Sure—that would be just great." Harper took her hand and helped her off the stool. It was soft and smooth. When she moved, he could smell her perfume. She was home, apple pie, and desire rolled into one. She didn't release his hand and held it until they reached the table. Harper thought that she deliberately brushed her body against him. He felt weak inside at the touch of a woman.

"Ben, this is Dorothy Goddard. She has consented to join us for dinner. She has a friend who will also be with us."

"Well, I am pleased to make your

acquaintance. It is refreshing to see one so beautiful as you in this land of ugliness. When is your friend arriving?"

"Actually she is here in the building—she just went downstairs to our apartment to wash up. Well here she is now." A short slim brown-haired girl approached the table. She had a beautiful smile which created dimples on her cheek.

"Joyce, this is Lieutenant Paul Harper. Isn't that right Paul." She turned and asked him, and before he could answer she introduced Benjeman.

"Glad to meet you both. I was downstairs taking a hot shower to remove the dust. I visited one of the hospital's this morning. The heat really got to me as usual. You both look like you have been out on the road for awhile."

"I am sorry, we didn't realize that we looked so bad. Is there a place up here where we can clean up?"

"Sure if you are lucky, you can get a room here for the night and shower until your hearts content. Say, Dorothy, why don't we go down to our place and let the boys clean up there. We can throw on some music and fix a couple of drinks and they can take a shower and put on the two robes I was going to send my father for Christmas. The place is a little messy, but it would just take a minute to clean up."

Benjeman shifted his weight in the chair. "Listen we don't want to put you out on our account. We can find a room some place and meet you back here if you would like."

"Heavens no—Joyce is right—let's go down to our place. After you clean up, we can go out and have dinner some place or even here on the roof. There is a beautiful view from here at night. You can watch the entire war raging around the city. It is like sitting in a giant movie theater. Do we have to twist your arms?"

Needless to say they didn't have to twist their arms at all. The four of them took the elevator down to the fourth floor to the girl's apartment. It was on the inside of the building, that is to say it overlooked an inner courtyard four stories below them. It had a living room with a built-in kitchen, two bedrooms, and one connecting bath. For decorations the girls used travel posters on the walls, and these were mixed with lacquer wood paintings that they had picked up on the local economy. All in all, it had the appearance of a college coed's apartment. At the far side of the living room, there was an entrance to the balcony overlooking the courtyard below. The bathroom had French plumbing. The overhead water tank worked on occasion. The shower water flowed into the same hole in the floor as did the toilet water and the sink. But it was the closest thing to civilization that could be found in the country. The bathroom had no door, only two curtains on each side of it connecting the bedrooms.

"You fellows better take the shower together because there won't be enough water for the two of you at this time of day," Dorothy said as she slipped on a record on the stereo set.

"What would you both like to drink? We will get it ready for you while you are getting cleaned up."

"How about a seven and seven," Benjeman said as he poked his head out of the curtain. Harper started the shower running and it went all over the entire floor in the bathroom. However the floor was slanted toward the toilet so that the water would run into the drain there.

The hot shower was possibly the greatest sensation that Harper had experienced in months. It was a wonderful and refreshing feeling to be really clean again. He dreaded the thought of putting on his dirty clothes again. It is the simple things of life that a man misses in field—the lack of these items are perhaps one of the greatest hardships besides being away from home and a real woman. Benjeman was next to him, and he began singing one of the songs from Camelot…"If ever I would leave you, it would be in spring time."

Paul took a towel off the rack on the wall and began to dry himself. Benjeman swore under his breath as the water had turned cold. Harper smiled and was happy that it hadn't happened to him. He called out to Dorothy that he was dry and that he needed his clothes. She pulled the curtain aside and gave him a robe to put on. He fastened it with a string. It was a yellow terrycloth robe.

He entered the bedroom. The shades were drawn. Music of Johnny Mathis was coming from the living room.

"Sit on the bed for a minute and I will give

you a back rub if you would like," she said. He sat on the bed and noticed that she was wearing some delightful perfume. The scent surrounded him. He felt desire pulsing within him. He laid on his stomach and her hands began to gently relax the muscles in his back and shoulders and arms. Her hair fell across his shoulders as she was working. She pulled his arms out of the sleeves of the robe and placed the robe across his bottom. He was naked from the waist on up. Paul closed his eyes and enjoyed the tingling sensation within him. She leaned over and kissed him on the back of the neck. Paul rolled on his side and pulled her down beside him. She yielded in his arms. Her lips were soft and moist and she opened her mouth as he kissed her. Paul found the hook on her brassiere and unfastened it. He brought his hand around her waist and slowly inched up her stomach. His hand went inside the bra, and it gave way. Her breast was beating as he caressed it. He slid his other hand under the belt on her skirt. She pulled her muscles in as his hand went down her smooth stomach and to the maiden forest below. With a slight tug the skirt slipped off. They were wrapped in each others arms in the ecstasy of love and passion. When it was all over they reached on the bedstead and took a cigarette and shared it. She was still lying naked in his arms. She was beautiful. Her skin was milky white except her face and neck which were tanned a light brown by the tropical sun. Each breast was a masterpiece of creation. Her body was young and supple and desiring. Paul didn't want to leave this place again. For him the war was a million miles away. The record had stopped playing in the living room. There was a sound in the other room and one of them had gotten up to change the record. Voices could be heard in the courtyard below. But, inside the bedroom, everything was dark and soft and warm…safe.

"Say, you guys are awfully quiet in there." Benjeman yelled out from the other bedroom.

"We were just wondering the same about you all. What do you say that we finish getting ready and go out for dinner. Since the view is supposed to be so great from the top of this place we can eat there or whatever the girls want to do." Harper turned and asked Dorothy what she wanted to do this evening. She didn't answer. She pulled his head to her breast. Paul kissed her and pulled the blanket from the bed over the two of them. He kissed each nipple and tugged gently with his teeth, and kissed her ears and neck and eyes. Finally he found the sweetness of her mouth again. She moaned for him to come over her again— she wanted more loving and fulfillment.

They fell asleep in each other's arms for awhile. The rays of the sun turned slowly into the shadows of the night. They were awakened by noise and laughing in the apartment next to theirs. The people were having a party and it had progressed out to the balcony. Someone had dropped a bottle and it had crashed to the pavement in the courtyard below. It must have been funny because someone was saying "Let's drop another one...come on, don't be a party dud...drop it."

Paul kissed her on the forehead and got off of the bed and began to put his clothes on. He heard the clink of glasses from the living room and the swizzle of ice as it knocked against the side of a glass. He went in without his shoes on. Joyce and Ben were lying on the couch talking and enjoying a highball.

"Well, we thought you lovers were never going to quit. We hope that you can tear yourselves away long enough to have a bite to eat upstairs before the dining room closes."

"Yeah, well you know how one thing leads to another, so to speak. I'll just get my shoes on and see if Dorothy is ready and we can go."

Paul walked back to the bedroom. Dorothy had just put on a brightly colored dress. It was a gay print and a mini skirt to boot. After exchanging a few words, the two couples went upstairs to the dining room. They enjoyed a steak dinner with all of the trimmings. Afterwards they went out to the bar and looked out at Saigon.

There were a million lights twinkling in the night. On the horizon, a yellow hue was lighting up the landscape. The VC had hit the Bien Hoa ammunition dump again. The air was shaken by an explosion. Dorothy said, "Let's dance."

Their two bodies moved to the rhythm as if they were one. They danced and twirled and dipped as if they had practiced for years. Ben and Joyce spent most of the evening at the table enjoying their drinks. Paul noticed that Joyce danced with a couple of other officers who had approached the table. He wondered if the two of them had hit it off as well as he had.

"Dorothy, can I stay with you tonight? It may be a long time before I can get in here again. I can promise that I will try to come as soon as I can." He held her more tightly and bent down and kissed her behind the ear. She looked up into his face and smiled and nodded her head in agreement

"Yes, you can stay," she whispered, "you can stay."

"Do you think Joyce and Ben are getting along all right? Perhaps they just aren't made for each other's company."

"No, Joyce has lots of friends—she has been here a lot longer than I have." She immediately saw the hurt look in Paul's face. She bit her lip and said, "Oh Paul; Paul, I am sorry I didn't mean it that way at all. This just doesn't happen on every date believe me. You have gone to college—you know what it is like to be a woman that loses her reputation. I trust that you can still respect me after today and tonight. But I needed you, and I felt that you had the same feeling. It doesn't have to be more than that in a situation like this. My God, one of us could die tomorrow. Me right here in the city, and you out there with your men. No, Paul, I am willing to give what I have to the right man. And you fit my ideal. But as adults, we don't necessarily have to go off the deep end. Look let's wait until Christmas, and we can get together then for sure. I just want to live today for today, and no more than that. Can you understand?"

"Dorothy, I understand, and that's fine." He didn't understand—not really. At first he thought that he had lucked out by finding her. Now he found himself jealous at the thought of her sleeping with another man—even a stranger to himself that he would never see and perhaps never know. How silly this whole situation was, he thought to himself.

Paul and Dorothy excused themselves first, and went back down to the apartment. Paul put a stack of records on the record player, and she opened two beers from the icebox. When Benjeman and Joyce came in about an hour later both beers were only half finished. They could hear whispers coming from the bedroom. Joyce turned off the record player and took Benjeman's hand and they went into the other bedroom.

In the morning, Paul thought of nothing but the idea of staying in the city for as long as possible and planning the next trip that he could take to Saigon. Finally the moment for parting arrived, and they all embraced at the door. Benjeman left twenty dollars to cover the cost of the liquor and food that they had eaten. Joyce took it. Paul looked shocked and then kissed his date good-bye again, Benjeman glanced at the money on the table. Paul still didn't get the message. So he took twenty more dollars out of his wallet and left it there for the girls. Dorothy blushed. Benjeman smiled an thought to himself—perhaps this was her first time for fun and profit.

So they left, and the girls went back upstairs to the bar, as it was getting near lunch time.

Chapter Eight
The Defector

Tuy Von was on her way to the market This was always part of the daily routine. It is as much a part of daily living as having children. Most people have no refrigeration for their food. Thus fresh meat and vegetables had to be purchased for each days meals. Tonight was going to be a special occasion. Roan was coming for dinner. She had seen him only once in two months after they found him sleeping along the river bed. He had needed a place to hide for two days. Later Tuy Von had found out that the District Chief had been murdered. She assumed then that Roan had taken some part in the episode.

The menu in the marketplace was as varied as the imagination. Brains; heart; kidney; liver; chops, eyes from dogs, monkeys, chicken, pigs, or cows. Tuy Von decided on a young chicken for the dinner. The old woman from whom she bought it took it out of a wicker basket and tied the feet together with a small piece of wire. She looked more and bought some bamboo shoots for salad and green to-matoes. At another vendor, she got a fresh pineapple. Thus loaded Tuy Von started back to her home. The chicken would squawk and shake its wings once in a while but there was no way that it could escape.

An Loi is a large rural town. The government considered it a safe area under pacification. So there was a revolutionary development team that worked in the area. It existed because the Viet Cong used An Loi as a rest area, and they had a hospital hidden in tunnels near the town itself. There was a reluctant coexistence between the two forces. During the day, the government controlled the village and at night the Viet Cong did. It was really no different there than in other areas that the government believes was pacified. Each side feigned strength—the government to win the support of the entire village and the Viet Cong to prove that the government was powerless against them. Thus every so often there was an incident, an act of terror, an act of revenge, useless destruction in what had become a civil war in which the ideals of both sides had become blurred by international complications and involvement. In short this struggle was in the 1960s what the Spanish Civil War was in the 1930s. The great powers tested methods, weapons, and ideology while the peasantry and the people suffered and died. The reason for the war became blurred and forgotten. Only death and despair remained. If all the suffering were confined in one spot, a river of tears would form. As the people went to market every day, so they lived their lives and so went their allegiance— to the power and to the man with the gun at that moment and on that day.

Tuy Von passed the village mayor's house. She heard from her father that he was the richest man in the area. The only reason he continued living and hadn't been killed like the others was because he paid high taxes to the Viet Cong intelligence network. But no one else had ever mentioned it before. She wished the fighting would stop and that peace would return to the land. Some of her girlfriends had joined the resistance movements months ago. None of them had ever been home again. She wondered what they were doing and what had happened to them. She wiped some sweat off her forehead with the sleeve of her shirt and continued on her way home.

Vo Van Sao, her father, was working in the backyard. He was shaving a piece of wood with a knife and trying to fit it into place to hold one of the wheels on the ox cart. He looked up when his daughter approached and nodded with his head and continued working on the wheel. He noticed that his daughter had been to the village marketplace. He missed his wife even after all these years. He longed to hear her movements and voice around the house. She had been killed by the French several years before. They had entered the village looking for Viet Minh. She had tried to run away and had been caught. Some of the soldiers had raped her, and after they were finished they had shot her. His hand slipped, and he cut himself with the knife. It was a minor cut. If only he had two hands, he thought to himself. But he had got even with the French. He had made land mines that destroyed them and their vehicles. But, in the end, he had made a mistake and had lost most of his arm as a result. Out of habit he felt his stomach. He had been wounded by the shrapnel there too. But in recent years, it didn't bother him any more.

He looked up from his work again. Only this time it was jeeps that got his attention. A line of American and Vietnamese jeeps were going towards the center of town. One soldier was addressing the people to come to the schoolhouse. There would be doctors and nurses there to look at the sick. They would give out medicine and health kits to the people. Sao watched the children run after the jeeps, each one yelling louder than the other. For them it meant candy, balloons, and perhaps T-shirts. Sao hated these intruders in his village. He knew that you could not buy the allegiance and loyalty of people with candy and a few pills. One day these men would come back to this village and rape the women and burn their homes to the ground. They must win the war, he thought to himself. They must win soon.

"Father, are the soldiers going to stay here long? Roan is coming to eat with us tonight. I hope nothing will happen to him," Tuy Von said to the old man.

"No, child, they will be gone before the sun sets. Otherwise they would have brought many more soldiers with them. They are afraid to stay anywhere at night except in their camps. Be not afraid, little one. Roan will get here safely. By now word has already reached their camp that the soldiers are here. They will all stay away until they leave this afternoon.

Sao reached into his pocket and took out a plastic package. He slowly opened it and reached in. He placed a cigarette in his mouth, rolled the package back up, and put it back in his pocket. Tuy Von went in the house and came back in a minute with a hot coal from the kitchen stove. Sao lit the cigarette and inhaled the smoke.

Roan was sitting on the edge of a bunker on the outer defense line of the camp. He had left the tunnel complex because Troung was getting moody again about the death of his wife. When that happened Roan found that it was advisable to leave him to his own thoughts—alone. Below him was the stream bed which twisted and turned through the jungle. Some seventy-five meters to the east it entered the rice fields. But here in the jungle a man could not see for more than a few feet and sometimes not even that far. The stream followed along the bottom of the ravine. Their position at the top gave them the advantage of any enemy advancing on foot. They could not penetrate the jungle so they had to follow the stream bed into the camp. There were mines placed along the side of the cliffs, and the men in the bunkers could roll grenades over the top without ever showing their heads. It would cost any enemy a lot of dead to get in here, he thought to himself. They were also protected from view from the air so that gunships could not ever pinpoint their position. It was all in all an ideal position. Each man had his own shelter in the sides of the bunkers so that it would take a direct hit from artillery to kill anyone.

Roan had his feet dangling over the edge of the bunker. His thoughts were turning to Tuy Von. He knew that sooner or later he must leave the resistance. He wanted to return to his studies and a life of peace. His hand went into his pocket and he pulled out a wrinkled piece of paper. It was blue, white, and orange with printing; that was his pass to freedom. He had picked it up in the jungle several weeks ago, right after they had killed the District Chief. A helicopter had broadcast a message and dropped leaflets in the area. Troung had had the men burn the leaflets when they found them, but Roan had kept one for himself. If he was caught with it—it meant his death. That was one thing with which the resistance did not fool around and that was defectors or anyone who was suspected of having it on his mind. He really wasn't sure why he had kept the thing because he could give himself up at any police station. This was some sort of added security. This was the written proof that he was a true defector and had taken the chance of being caught with the evidence in his possession.

Roan caught the noise of footsteps in the water. They made a slashing noise. He quickly jumped behind the bunker and grabbed his rifle. Silently the word was passed along down the line that someone was approaching the camp. Men crawled to their positions in dead silence. Finally a figure appeared in the stream. It was one of the boys from the village who brought them news and served as a scout in the area. Everyone breathed a sigh of relief. The boy passed Roan's position and continued down the stream. About twenty meters from his position the stream made another sharp curve to the left. It was here that you entered the camp. Footholds were dug into the side of the cliff so that you could reach the top. This position was covered from the other side by a hidden machine gun position that was in a shallow cave on the other side of the stream some three quarters of the way to the top of the cliff. Since there was no danger, men could be heard talking and joking once again.

Troung was sitting in the tunnel looking at a model of the American base camp at Bien Hoa. He was studying all of the avenues of approach to the camp and the ones that provided the most amount of concealment and yet provided easy access and exit for fast movement during the night. He was also plotting his mortar positions in relation to the airfield. It was at this point that he heard someone was approaching the area. He pulled down the outside covering on the tunnel which immediately cut off the light supply. At this point, he lit a candle and moved back into the tunnel some thirty meters until he reached another escape route. This was right before the entrance to the hospital. He poked his head into the section and gave them the warning that someone was approaching. Immediately the patients were made ready for evacuation. If it was Americans and they used gas in the tunnel they would all have to leave within a few seconds or they would suffocate to death.

A guard poked his head into the tunnel and informed them that everything was all right. Troung returned to his position, and as he got there, the boy from the village was waiting to see him.

"Well, are you the one who caused us all this worry?"

"Captain?"

"Yes, I am in command here. What can I do for you?"

"The Americans have just entered the village and they bring doctors with them. I thought that you should know about it."

"Good news. Pass the word among our friends to go and see them. Have them all bring the medicine to you after they leave, and you can bring it back to us. Perhaps you will soon be old enough to join us. What do you say to that?"

"Can I have a gun too like all of the others?"

"Yes, you will have that and more. Perhaps I will let you carry the rockets that we are going to use against the enemy." Then Troung dismissed the young boy to go back to the village and carry out his task.

Roan was back sitting on the edge of the bunker when the young boy from the village passed below him in the water. He was thinking about his meeting with Tuy Von for dinner. He wondered if he could trust her with his decision of leaving the Viet Cong. Roan knew that her father would betray him without batting an eye. But his daughter seemed to be different. She had not inherited the revolutionary spirit of the old man, of that he was sure. Perhaps she would even become his wife, he thought to himself. She could leave with him. But that was dangerous too because she would be questioned and she might be forced to tell about her father's activities for the resistance. No, that would be a poor idea.

He had been able to get word to her that he would come for dinner just a week ago. It was almost impossible to leave the camp without Troung's permission. After they hit the District Chief, they hadn't come directly to the camp because of the hospital. So they all had stayed in the village. The only reason he was getting away tonight was because Troung trusted him completely. That was the mistake of all men; believing that man was not infallible. Perhaps he too would make that same mistake under different circumstances.

Slowly the heat of the day passed away. Gradually the coolness of the night descended upon them in the jungle. Roan slipped on his shirt and put his rifle down. He picked it up again. He would miss it he thought to himself. It had become part of him like an extension of his body. He depended on it for survival in the world. He put it down once again. This had been the deciding factor of his defection. He abhorred death and suffering. Neither side was right. But leaving the Viet Cong he could find peace and be kept in some camp until the war was over. He could sleep nights like a human being and not like a cunning animal which waits for the shadows of the night to move. His body would no longer be jarred to his soul by the impact of an exploding shell as it rained down steel and lead upon him and his friends. Yes he would now quit the war and have peace an freedom from the fear of death in an unmarked grave where he would not be worshipped by his family as he had worshipped his ancestors.

He followed the trench system around until he reached the path down to the stream bed. He slowly began to inch his way down towards the stream.

"Where are you going, Roan?"

The voice came from behind him. It was Troung. Roan froze where he stood. He began to sweat. He was afraid that he would give himself away.

"I am going to see Tuy Von for dinner. I shall be back in the morning. You told me that I could go."

"Listen, while you are in the village, find the boy who was here this afternoon. Make sure that we get the medicine that he was going to bring to me. Have a good night, my friend."

"I will—thank you."

Roan reached the stream bed and began his trip to the village. Every step that he took was like a burden being taken off of his back. At last he was going to be free. For one short minute he thought that all of his plans would be in vain and that he would never be able to get away from them.

Slowly he made his way down the stream. His feet could not move fast enough. He felt like he was in a dream and was being chased. Every once in a while, he would look back over his shoulder to see if he was being followed. But, there was no one there—nothing there except his past, and that he was going to escape now, no matter what the end result may be. He could not go back; they would be suspicious.

Finally he reached the rice fields. He began to walk along the dikes to dry himself out before he reached the village. Roan ran about seventy meters to get behind some farmers who were returning home for the night. When he reached the village, he headed directly for Tuy Von's house.

She was waiting for him and the dinner was ready on the table. When her father was not looking, he kissed her gently on the cheek. She put her hand on his shoulder and yielded to him with her eyes.

After dinner he decided to throw all caution to the wind. He confided his plan to her. She could meet him in one month at the Chieu Hoi camp for defectors. They could be married, and when he could leave they would take a bus to Nha Trang where he would begin school again.

Tuy Von said nothing. Her lack of words and the love in her eyes spoke the words that did not come from her lips. The plan was sealed. The man who had been a student in the university, a soldier, a Viet Cong, and now a defector was going to begin life again.

He kissed her good-bye and headed for the police station in the center of the village. He thought better of it and began to go in the opposite direction towards Phu Loi and the police station there. It was also the location of the defector center.

Chapter Nine
Binh Doung Chieu Hoi

In what was once a cemetery for the political victims of the Diem regime in the late 1950s, there was now a province defector center. It rested behind the subsector headquarters of the government. While the buildings were relatively new, they had become old from lack of attention and repair. Pigs and chickens roamed the yard. Flies infested the area around the public latrine which was situated next to the kitchen. There was usually one or two armed guards at the front gate. They rested inside a sandbagged bunker. The rear and both sides of the camp had various sized bunkers manned at all times by determined soldiers. They were different by the fact that they were all loyal Viet Cong soldiers only weeks or days ago. Now they were ready to kill their former comrades at any time and any place. They had a zeal for their new position—men who must prove their loyalty to the firm without any reservation or doubt.

Harper was taking all of these thoughts and

sights in as his interpreter was telling him about the camp. They were sitting in the interrogation room which was at the west end of the main administration building with a view of most of the camp. There were gun slits in the walls in case of attack from the outside. Harper had been sitting around the office that morning waiting for something to happen when they got word that a defector had arrived from B-40. Since there was no IPW team in the area, Lancaster had sent him to the camp to find out what had happened. They were waiting to see Phan van Roan. He was rumored to be the executive officer of B-40 and it was known that he was at least in the high echelon of the force.

Captain Nichols was standing by back at the camp with his tape equipment to get a message from this man and play it back over his area of operation and his base camp to induce other members of his group to defect to the government.

Harper had one class in interrogation while attending school in the states. It had lasted one day. But since he was the man available, he got picked for the job. He fumbled for his pack of cigarettes. He would be facing the enemy from across the table, and he did not know what he should ask this man or even where to begin.

The Chieu Hoi chief entered the door of the office. He introduced himself as Mr. Quay. Behind him was a short individual wearing a white sport shirt and black pants. His feet were bare and were marked by long use without shoes in the jungle. They were cut, deformed, and infected in the toes by long unattended cuts. His head was bowed and he looked as if he were ashamed. He stood in front of Harper's desk, hat in hand. Harper told him to be seated. To break the ice, he offered the man a cigarette.

The two men sat there facing each other and neither one said a word to the other. Finally Harper asked him his name, rank, and unit. And so the interrogation began. In the beginning it was a question of which one was more cunning than the other. Slowly Roan realized that he was not going to be harmed and that the American facing him was kind at heart. This, in fact, gave him, Roan, the advantage. He could lead his interrogator where he wanted by the answers he gave to his questions. However he had to be careful so as not to antagonize the American. In the end, he began to supply the information that the American needed. It was at this point that he let it be known that his command of English was not bad at all and that he could understand most of the questions before they went through the interpreter.

Roan found himself faced with a large moral problem of completely selling out his former comrades. To have left the resistance did not, in fact, bother him in the least, for this was something which he had planned to do for weeks. But to deliberately cause the death of his old friends was something which he had not thought about. This was a crisis point that he had not planned on facing. At this time, Harper seemed to grasp the situation.

"Roan, if you are worried that the Viet Cong will kill you if you give us the information that we need, you do not have to worry about that because we will protect you. If the information that you have is of great enough value, we can take you out of this camp for a period of time and let you live with us in our camp. We would, in fact, provide you with a job. Now is that what you are worrying about?"

Roan simply said, "Yes." He then began to tell all that he knew about the organization.

B-40 is presently located in the An Loi jungle area. If you have a map, I can show you the exact area to search. They had eighty-three men in the area when I left. All these men were armed with light weapons. We did have three 60mm mortars.

"The weapons platoon also had two rocket launchers which could knock out any tank that we could put in the field. There were many men in the hospital itself. They were being treated for wounds and sickness. They could all be evacuated at very short notice. The entire complex is under the ground in a series of tunnels. These tunnels are guarded by a complex bunker system. To get into the area, a land force would have to follow the stream bed and would place themselves in a dangerous position because they could be ambushed. Now if you look at the map, you leave An Loi by this route and you cross the rice fields at this point behind this large house here. Then you proceed to the woodline where you will pick up the stream about here on your map. Now there is no difficulty going up the stream bed, the water is never more than waist deep at this time of the year. Now our camp is about seventy-five meters inside the jungle. But the problem for any force that you send in is that it is situated on the top of the stream beds. It is impossible to reach over land because the jungle is so thick. We could drop grenades and fire at troops without ever exposing our positions. We could never see the planes overhead—we could hear them, of course, but they could not see us either. Thus you would not have air support. You could not call artillery once you were in there because you could not direct the fire of it."

Harper was amazed that this man knew so much about the area. He excused himself for a moment and went outside to ask Captain Nichols on the radio to come down to the center. He thought with both of them working on the man they could extract more information in a shorter period of time. Besides with Nichols here Roan would be more committed than before because he would be put on tape and it would be flown back over the area that his friends were living. Harper decided to ask him what their group knew about the allied troops in the area. He left his radio and went back inside the room.

"What does you commander know about our troops operating in this area?"

"When I was there he knew everything. I

listened to your radios and reported all of your movements to him."

"Does anyone else in the company know enough English to accomplish the same mission that you did?"

"It is possible. But I did not know anyone else. I know that you operated on 63.10 for your operations, that the division net was 49.30, that your dust-off was 66.00, the advisors here worked on 38.30, and so forth. Yes we knew every move you were going to make. We only acquired this knowledge in recent weeks since we ambushed the District Chief and got his radio. It was some how intact after we ambushed the jeep. If I had stayed with the unit, you can be sure that we would be waiting for you if you had planned to come into our area. When you had smaller operations, we had time to send runners to other areas to warn them that your troops were coming."

"Would you like a Coke? It is really getting warm in here. Besides I realize that it is getting near your lunch period," Harper said. He got up and took a cigarette and offered one to Roan. Harper sat on the corner of the desk and enjoyed the first puff and inhaled the smoke into his lungs. He realized that there should really be a professional interrogator here getting all of the facts from this man. He had an individual in his possession that knew more about his division than he knew. This man must be questioned by higher authorities. He would be of tremendous value to the allies if we used him correctly, Harper thought to himself.

A jeep entered the front of the yard; it was followed closely by a huge cloud of red dust that settled over the occupants of the jeep once they stopped in front of the administration building. Captain Nichols and Hannaman got out of the jeep

"Well I see you have a new helper today, sir!"

"Not exactly, buddy. Sergeant Hannaman came along because you have a new mission. I will use your interpreter while you two go down to sector house in Phu Coung and talk to a prisoner that was picked up this morning. You will be able to use one of their interpreters there. When you finish you can drop back here and pick us up. It looks like we may go into An Loi with a bang tonight or first thing in the morning. Now introduce me to this fellow, and we will be all set."

Harper introduced the two men and left the camp with Hannaman and headed towards the Province Capital to see what was up there. He assumed that he would be briefed on the situation once he was there. He would get a hold of Captain Jefferies the S-2 and find out what was happening.

Sector headquarters in any province is the seat of military and political power. It worked directly with the Vietnamese province chief which is usually a Colonel in the South Vietnamese Army. The actual compounds of the

Capital building and the military headquarters may be separated but in reality they are one in the same. The government depends on the military for survival. The army is the arm of the government and the government is the voice of the army. Democracy exists only on paper. It exists at the whim of military power and martial law. It is there for convenience. It covers up graft and corruption through legality and mounds of unrelated paperwork to turn the trail cold when there is a popular outcry of inefficiency and waste.

Jefferies was a redheaded captain, short and slimly built and just recently promoted. He was from New Jersey and was glad that it was a place from which he was and not to which he was going back. He was an intelligent man and in his spare time he took out the long range patrols for kicks. He had developed a slight stutter, something which was common for a man continually exposed to danger in this country. A stutter after all gives a man a slight chance to change his mind in the middle of a sentence or to change his course of action. In short he was military—a man of decision and a man of contradictions.

Jefferies was standing on the steps of the main entrance to the headquarters building talking to a Vietnamese captain. His feet were apart and a rifle hung from his shoulder. He was wearing a cloth hat instead of a helmet and it sat on a jaunty angle on his head, more in defiance than for protection against the sun.

"Good afternoon, sir. The sergeant and I

have come to see you about some prisoner that you have picked up. That is the extent of my information. Would you mind filling me in on the details?"

"Lieutenant, I would be more than happy to. However the old man is unhappy with you people. It seems that you are always planning operations without consulting him. You people take all of the publicity. After all this is our war too, you know. So you are going to fill me in on this character from B-40 before we go further. Besides the Charlie that we picked up last night is wounded and is being questioned by Captain Lon's men at the present time. After they are finished, we will give him some medical treatment and then you can have him. Now why don't you come into my office and let's talk about the problem."

The office was in a corner of the building on the first floor which is the second floor in this country. There were wooden shutters opening out on both corner walls that overlook the courtyard. Against one was a wooden desk and above it was a map of the province filled with stickers and notations. There were two extra chairs in the room and a field phone on the desk. Hung next to the map was a communist flag of South Vietnam and on it is a Chinese automatic rifle. The flag was stained with blood, a reminder of some past victory and the agony of its defender.

"Here are my notes, sir, from the interrogation. As you can see, a fellow by the name of

Troung is the commander of the force. It looks to me as if this fellow Roan was the second or third in command. I know that he played a part in the murder of the District Chief. I also have found out according to him that they currently have eighty-three men in the unit, and as you can see, here is the list of weapons that they have. In short they are a formidable force to reckon with if we go into this area. Now if you look at the map, I can show you where they are located at the present time. Unless, of course, they have left when this man defected." Harper stood up and walked to the map. "They are located in this jungle area just a stone throw from An Loi. He suggests that we use this house as a point of reference and enter the jungle at about this point here. There is a stream that can be used to get to the base camp. According to him, it is the only way to get in there. The camp is some seventy-five meters into the jungle itself. It would seem as if the villagers have been completely aware of its presence for a long time. Now, I think that…"

"That is enough for now, Harper. I believe that I have enough information to pass on to the old man. Let's go and see how our prisoner is doing. You might be interested to know that he is also from An Loi. We caught him outside the village last night with explosives. He claims that he was a forced laborer for the Viet Cong. But, regardless, he was caught with the goods on him and no one was with him to our knowledge."

The interrogation building was a separate part of the compound. The hallways were lighted by hanging light bulbs. The windows were closed and were draped with black cloth to keep the light out. At the end of a corridor was one of the interrogation rooms. On the floor a man was lying—he was tied like a pig for slaughter. That is to say, his hands were tied behind him and his feet were raised in the air and were tied to his hands. The rope then continued to his neck where if the man struggled he choked himself to death. In the room there was a Vietnamese warrant officer and two sergeants—they took turns beating the man on the back of his legs and arms with a long supple piece of bamboo. Everything was done slowly and deliberately and without hurry; they had all the time in the world. The man was bleeding from a flesh wound in the shoulder. His capturers offered him medical treatment if he gave them the information that they desired. The three men smiled as Harper, Hannaman, and Jefferies entered the room. They enjoyed their job. It was, in fact, their primary duty to interrogate the prisoners. They were men with long practice at this sort of thing and they always got their information. They had yet to fail. Even the most dedicated Viet Cong would talk eventually. It only took different types of methods to meet each situation.

"He still insists that he is only a forced laborer, sir," the sergeant stated while wiping the sweat from his forehead with his sleeve.

"Offer to accept that and that we will untie him if he tells us where their camp is outside of An Loi. Tell him his jail sentence will be lesser if we turn him over as a forced laborer. We must be certain, sergeant, about the location of the VC base camp in the area. If he lies to us we will know it. We will wait in my office for an answer. Carry on."

"Yes, sir."

As they left the warrant officer was bending over and speaking softly into the man's ear. As he was talking, one of the sergeants hit the man again with his stick on the wound on his shoulder. His groan could be heard all the way down the hall.

Outside the building children were playing in the yard. They were dependents of the officers and men living in the compound. They were pointing sticks at one another and playing war games in the yard. Their fathers in the buildings around them were playing for real. At times it was hard to distinguish one from the other.

The three men went into the coffee shop and ordered French coffee. It was a thick substance weakened and sweetened by heavy cream and sugar. Behind the coffee shop there were barriers of barbed wire and beyond that were rice fields. Harper looked out and studied the landscape and watched the farmers work their land. The war seemed so far away from them, and yet they were within a short rifle shot of it. It surrounded them in anything that they did and wherever they went. He wondered how many of them were guerillas by night and farmers by day. How many had sons and relatives fighting on both sides of the conflict? Perhaps most if not all, and he knew it. Non-involvement was the best way to live and yet each man could not escape becoming involved. He might be spared for months or even years, but eventually he must make a commitment, and if he was wrong he was dead. That was a horrible way to have to live, not knowing which side he would have to face in the morning or which would come to his door in the dead of night.

Jefferies was talking about Bob Hunter, the CIA man who was always running over for information. "Listen, they are always after the strangest information. But it doesn't make any difference to me because he has great parties over at his place. Have you been there? He has Chinese mercenaries for guards. They are the toughest little bastards that I have ever seen. They would rather shoot you than look at you, and that is no lie. Christ, they are armed to the teeth. I am glad that they are on our side, that's for sure. Have you ever seen the other troops they have? All the men are former officers or NCO's from the Vietnamese army. They elect their own officers and they are all professionals. I hear that many of them have committed crimes of one sort or another. I met a lieutenant who had eleven prisoners in his care. So he gets drunk one night and goes out and kills every one of them—including two women. Well, anyway, he used his knife and slit their throats. The story goes that a couple of the prisoners were influential in the government even though they were VC, so the lieutenant lost his commission and got booted out of the army. Then one day, he ends up in their outfit. I actually talked to the guy—he was the mess officer of the company."

"How long will it take to get the information from the prisoner, sir?" Hannaman asked.

"Not long, sergeant. My men usually can extract the information that they want to know in a relatively short period of time. The problem is that the little bastards are generally so dedicated that they don't talk at all. But our people have ways of overcoming the problem. Sometimes it isn't necessary to lay a hand on them. Just the threat of force is enough. Another will sell out for money or personal gain. Each man is an individual case. I personally don't agree with all of the methods used, but as in anything else you can get used to it. Here it is a part of daily life. Life is torture and suffering in this country. People seem immune to pain itself. I have seen people with wounds that make me scream inside with agony. But they don't even bat an eye. They have a very fatalist attitude in this country. The closest thing I ever saw to it is the attitude of the Peruvian Indians. I lived there with my father when he was a military attaché."

As they were talking, the little sergeant who had spoken to them before entered the coffee shop. He was still smiling. The gold on his teeth showed as he smiled and spoke.

"Captain, the man says that there is a VC base camp in the jungle near the village. He cannot point it out on the map, as he cannot read. He is willing to take us there if we go to the village. He mentioned that it is near a stream. However he states that he has never been in the camp itself. Do you want us to question him some more or give him to the national police?"

"Have the doctor look at his wound. We will keep him for a while. I am not ready to turn him over to the police yet."

"Well, captain, our information is confirmed. I will be getting back to camp. Perhaps we will be seeing you later on tonight or in the morning."

"Sure enough. Take it easy on the way back."

"Right, sir." Harper saluted and left. Hannaman started the jeep and they were on their way once again.

"Where to, lieutenant?"

"We have to stop at the Chieu Hoi center and pick up Nichols and the VC—then we will head back for camp."

Chapter Ten
The Festival

It was raining outside, and the water hit the tin roof of the briefing room like falling stones on a snare drum. The wind was blowing, sending in a fine mist of water through the screens. The bamboo and grass curtains rattled and swung back and forth against the walls. The coolness of the air and wind felt good to the hot and dirty men assembled in the room. They were huddled together exchanging glances, smoking and watching Major Lancaster at the map board.

"The reason for the short fuse on this operation is simply because we got a defector from B-40 last night. If intelligence is correct, the VC are still in the area and may not be aware that one of their men have left yet. Sector has also picked up a forced laborer, and he confirms the information that we already have. Both of these men are willing to go in with us and point out both the base camp and Viet Cong themselves. Our medical team was in here just a few days ago and they reported that there are very few men in the village itself. We can assume that the VC must be operating in force in the entire area. We have not contacted the Vietnamese Revolutionary Development team in the village simply because we cannot be positive of their loyalty at the present time." Lancaster shifted on his feet, and scratched his neck with his hand, and turned toward the crowd of men gathered there. "Captain Luttner, you brief the men on the entire intelligence picture and show them the air photos that you have of the village."

"Gentlemen, this is the situation as we see it at the present time…" Luttner took a breath and began his briefing to the men. "I believe that you can expect to find somewhere in the neighborhood of ninety to one hundred thirty Viet Cong in the immediate area of An Loi. We know that some eighty to ninety of these men are part of B-40 which is located in the jungle here. There are a large number of their causalities in a hospital in the area. The exact amount we do not know for sure. There is also a village local force VC group. You can expect all of the roads to be mined. You can assume that the safe way to travel is to follow the ox cart paths—but be careful here too. The main roads could be mined, especially at junctions and along the sides of the road. Watch the children—if they are staying away from any area proceed with extreme caution. We know that they are equipped with mortars—three to be exact, and they have anti-tank capability with a rocket launcher. Most of the men are carrying

Chinese automatic weapons at the present time. Thus they are a formidable enemy. This is going to be a combined operation—so remember and think before you start shooting. Lieutenant Harper is going to have the honor of taking out the Chieu Hoi company on this operation. It has already been cleared through the sector people. All of these men have been Viet Cong in the past. They have all been battle-tested on our side. There will be some one hundred twenty of them going in with us. They will be the first ones into the jungle area. They all wear the black uniforms, so be careful at whom you shoot. I can't emphasize this enough."

Harper's mouth dropped open and a look of disbelief overcame his face. All eyes of those around him sought him out for a comment, but he said nothing. The impact of Luttner's statement was still registering on his mind. Before he could register a question, Captain Luttner stepped down and Captain Lundgren took his place.

"The operation will kick off at 0515 tomorrow. The ARVN are going to surround the village with two mechanized infantry companies. At 0530 we will link up at the south entrance to the village and drive north, searching the homes. Simultaneously Harper and his contingent will head for the jungle and the base camp. He will be followed by one US infantry company. There will be an artillery strike on the jungle at 0515—this will last for fifteen minutes. When it lifts, the search of all areas begins. We will be leaving the compound at 0400 by armored convoy. Each man is to draw two days rations and double his basic load of ammunition and two canteens of water. At 0730 the festival element will enter the village. This is going to be a complete festival. This will divert the children and the old people while we interrogate and search the homes more thoroughly during the day. Thus medical teams, mobile kitchens for a lunch meal, entertainment, movies, and so forth will be in the village for the complete show. This entire operation has got to be a success because we have word the press is going to show up for this one. This will probably mean that the commanding general will also arrive on the scene."

"Which brings in another point that should be brought up at this time." Lancaster stepped to the front again. "Since the Vietnamese are going in with us on this operation, they are going to be responsible for the interrogation of all the prisoners. Stay clear of that area and make sure that the newsmen don't get in there with them. They will be using one room of the schoolhouse for their mission."

Lancaster waited a minute for the words to sink in, then he continued. "Nichols, you will be flying the psy-war ship beginning at 0530 over the village. You will be playing the tape from the defector initially. Later in the morning, you can play the assembly tape for the hamlet festival. I will let you know when to begin. Harper, initially the defector will be going in with you to the jungle. As we collect prisoners, we will bring him out for identification of them. Later in the morning, you will be working with Captain Luttner in the interrogation room. This is presuming that you don't run into heavy contact in the base camp. I believe that they may have left as of tonight. We can't be sure of course. Another point— we have to pick up this man's girlfriend as part of the deal. So you, Harper, will be responsible for this later in the day. Unless there are any questions at this time, you may all go home to bed. I want the S-2 and S-3 to stay while we go over the order of march and some other points for the morning. Good night, gentlemen."

The men filed out of the room into the rain and their own thoughts. Some would head for the bar and console themselves with drinks and talk about women, home, years past, and a lot of things they really never had. Still others would feel compelled to write a letter home to a loved one, wife, mother, father, or son. In each case, every man would be lost and alone with his own thoughts. Tomorrow they would all be together functioning and acting as one individual, as the military machine that they were.

Hannaman hurried past a few of his friends and came up behind Harper.

"Sir," he said with a slight hesitation.

Harper slowed down and looked around to see his friend there.

"Yes, sergeant? How is it going?"

"I was wondering, sir, what my job would be tomorrow. Do you want me to go with you?"

"Right, Sarge. Get ready to go with me and pick up Taylor for our radio operator. This is going to be some operation. You and I out there with a 120 former VC and all of them armed to the teeth. This is sure a new twist to the war."

"It's a real ball buster, Lieutenant. Shit. We'll do all right as long as that artillery is going in before us. Besides the sector people have had these guys out before and nothing has happened to doubt their sincerity. I heard that they have taken causalities in the past. So we should be okay with them, sir."

"We will know soon enough, sergeant. See you in the morning."

"Goodnight, sir." Hannaman disappeared into the darkness and the rain.

Harper walked on towards his tent. Voices, lights, and sounds of men at war all came to his ears from the mystery of the surrounding shadows. The sky was void of stars this night. Heavy, swirling clouds swam past the rays of the moon, one after another in an endless parade of forms and designs.

In the darkness Harper tripped over a taut rope. He fell to one knee. He swore and continued on his way. Somewhere on the edge of the perimeter a flare lit up the area. Everything assumed ghostly shadows, then all was dark again. Someone's dog barked nearby. For a few seconds the clouds left the moon uncovered. Harper saw the familiar outline of his tent near the road. He entered and threw the canvas flap aside. After striking a match, his hand was able to find the single light bulb in the tent. The bare bulb glared down and blinded his eyes briefly. He looked around and found that he was alone. His teammates must be at the club, he thought to himself.

The white towel felt good on his wet and dirty face. He held it there to let the coolness of the cloth sink into his pores. He placed it back on a nail pounded into one of the indoor tent supports. As he sat on the bed, his voice let out a small sigh of relief. Tired muscles and a tired man were going to rest while the mind continued to work and think and dream about events to come and days past.

The cot was wet and cool on his body. Dampness never left anything. He pulled the poncho liner up around his head and began to slowly fall asleep. The sound of the artillery batteries on the other side of the camp seemed to fit into his dream. Gradually the echoes of each blast approached nearer and nearer to his tent. It was then that Harper's unconscious mind made the distinction between the outgoing woompf of the artillery and the incoming sounds of kroompf of enemy mortar shells. Instantly he rolled out of the cot. He became entangled in the mosquito netting. He ripped it apart to get loose. Crouching low he grabbed his helmet, weapon, and web belt, in that order. He whirled around and ran out the back of the tent and rolled into the culvert along the side of the dirt road. Figures could be seen running in all directions. The entire sky was now lit up by flares and fires. They hit the airstrip, he thought to himself. Taking a look up and down the road, he saw that it would be safe to dash to the bunker across the street. Holding on to his helmet with one hand and carrying his equipment in the other, he made a straight run for the bunker. There was a tremendous explosion to his left. He could hear the screams of men. The gasoline truck behind the officers club had been hit. The entire structure was enveloped in flames. A figure darted out from the flames and he was on fire. You could not hear his screams above the noise and screams of others.

"Comin' through," he yelled and dove through the door of the bunker.

Someone shined a flashlight in his face. The soldier inquired who he was.

"Lieutenant Harper. Are there any medics in here? If so get your ass over to the club— they need help there. The rest of you will follow me to the inner perimeter so we can boost up the strength at those bunkers."

The noise and din of the war as around all of them as they ran from the door of the bunker. Men dressed in a shirt, some with only their boots, others with only their pants, but they all had their weapons and a helmet. They were conditioned to their surroundings like Pavlov's dog. When the gong sounded, they need not be reminded what they were to do or what would be expected from them. It was their job, and they were paid for it.

They ran and crouched in single file. Ahead of them the dim outline of a bunker was visible. There was activity of men outside of it in the rear. As they got closer someone yelled at them to halt and give the password.

"Jesus Christ, we don't know the password. I am Lieutenant Harper and my mission is to reinforce you position up here. Can you hear me?"

"Sure, come on up."

Harper rose from the ground and continued up the slope to the bunkers. He began to hear the machine gun firing from the first line of bunkers on the other side of the slope near the bottom. As he approached the top, he could see tracers seeking out targets in the night.

"What's the picture like out there?"

It was Bob DeVries, a new man who had recently joined the unit. He lived in the tent next to Harper's and had guard duty that night.

"Well, Paul, the word that I got is that we have a company-sized ambush out there, and they got ambushed and Charlie is trying to overrun them. They are getting support from the gunships. There, there is one now." There was a burst of light from the sky—then came the muffled sound of the mini-guns from the helicopter. Harper could see that they were circling in pairs, one at low level with lights on acting as a decoy and another close behind it with no light at all until they found a target. The ground shook under them as the heavy mortar from the base began a preselected pattern of fire along the perimeter. Dirt and cold steel flew in all directions.

"Where do you want these men?"

"Have them go in pairs along the line. The password is night owl."

"Okay, guys, you got the word—take off."

"They got the club, Bob; I hope we didn't lose too many guys tonight. They never had a chance if they were in there."

"Yeah, Paul, I saw it get hit; I was looking that way when it happened. Come on inside while I make a commo check with my bunkers."

"Sarge, check with the bunkers and remind them not to fire unless I give the word. Our mission is to cover the guys down below us and prevent Charlie from reaching the final defense line behind us. Remind those jokers of the fact and that we have people out there. Unless something drastic happens they are not going to have any targets to shoot at."

"Right, sir. Lightning eleven, this is lightning six—romeo—over."

Suddenly just as quickly as it had began all was quiet except for the droning of the aircraft overhead and the yells of men putting out fires and calling for medics. The enemy had retreated for another day or another night. He went back to his lair in the jungle to hide and regroup and plan for his next operation.

The bunker was dark and musty. Fred bummed a cigarette from DeVries. He shielded the flame from his lighter in his helmet. He passed the cigarette to the sergeant and he took a deep drag. He was still contacting all of the bunkers along their line. Flares were still going off along the entire perimeter and would for the rest of the night as the men down on the line were edgy. Besides there were the constant rumors that the VC had dug tunnels that would surface behind the bunkers. In situations like that, it was hard not to be edgy at night. Every shadow was an enemy, and you took no chances or you were a dead man. Once darkness set in no one would even visit the bunkers down below—it was an unofficial no-man's land. Each bunker had three or four men, and one was detailed to cover the rear. So friendly troops stayed away at night unless a visit was coordinated and cleared all the way down the line.

Finally the reserve force got the word to return back to their normal duties. For Harper that was bed, and he welcomed the idea with relish. He decided not to go to the office to avoid any details at this hour of the night. If they wanted him, they knew where he lived. He said goodnight to DeVries and headed down the slope to his tent. The officer's club was still burning. He avoided his curiosity and went straight back to his tent. Any job left there was for medics and engineers and he was neither.

Once again the coolness of his bed felt good. He didn't bother to put his mosquito net back up again. Harper fell asleep instantly.

Harper, Hannaman, and Taylor were riding in

one of the two and a half ton trucks with the Chieu Hoi Company. Actually the entire company could be crammed into two trucks with all of their equipment. The road was still dark. The moisture of the previous night prevented large clouds of dust from blowing in their faces. Looking up and down the line, one could see men crouched behind their machine guns on the gun jeeps, staring and listening into the darkness. Radio antennas swung back and forth with movement of the vehicle. Each truck and jeep looked like a porcupine with the rifle barrels of men protruding from the sides in all directions.

Harper was thinking about the raid the night before. The aviation company had taken the brunt of the attack. They had, however, lost six men in the officer's club in their area last night. One had been a Vietnamese waiter. The other five were officers. They were all in critical condition in the hospital. Harper was grateful that none of their section had been injured in the attack. His roommates had been playing poker in another tent when the attack had hit. They had made it through without a scratch. In the confusion someone had made off with the money and winnings on the table. There are even thieves among friends.

Harper looked at the two men sitting next to him in the truck. Minh and Roan were speaking together in low tones. He wondered if the information that this man had given and which was the basis of the entire operation was accurate and correct. How many men's lives depended on this one man and his story. Would they all be walking into a trap deep in the jungle from which there would be no return for any of them? Paul had no love for the defectors at this point. To say the least, he was very concerned about the whole situation. He actually had only three men around him who he could trust, and in this situation that was not very good odds.

His thoughts were interrupted by the sound of artillery fire landing in the jungle somewhere to their front. Instantly all the men began to tense up and there was silence in the convoy except for the chattering on the radios. In a few minutes, they came to a stop in a wooded area along the road. The word was passed down from the front of the convoy to dismount the vehicles and proceed on foot from herein. Quickly the men left the vehicles and deployed themselves along each side of the road. They lay there flat on their stomachs awaiting orders to proceed on their missions. Every eye and every gun searched the morning dawn for signs of the enemy. Thus far except for the artillery, all was quiet.

"Sergeant Minh, explain to each of the platoon leaders that we are going to cross the rice fields with each platoon going in on line. Each element will be thirty yards apart. We will go with the first platoon. We will regroup at the stream bed and send the second platoon in first with the Chieu Hoi, then the first platoon and third and fourth. Since it will be impossible to have flank protection we will go in columns up the stream bed by platoon. Make sure that they understand this. I want no deviation from this procedure.

"Yes, sir, I will have them follow your instructions." Minh raised himself and began going down the road to inform the different platoon leaders. The artillery was still crashing into the jungle with muffled explosions as it hit the ground. Harper heard the drone of a chopper overhead. That would be Nichols, he thought to himself. From his position and the bend in the road he still could not see the village itself. In the branches of the trees overhead birds were stirring and fluttering and flying away with each crash of an artillery shell. Paul was watching the birds when Hannaman spoke to him.

"I've got six on the horn, and he says to move out on the double. We should have already been to the edge of the jungle."

"Give him a Wilco out, sarge."

Harper rose to his feet and made a circling motion with his hand and began walking in a northwest direction past the edge of the woods and into the rice paddies. Men were moving up behind him. Gradually the wavering line began to straighten itself out. Every man was preoccupied with the sound of his own feet as they sloshed through the rice paddies and over the small dikes and back into the water once again. The village was clearly visible now on their right. Men were running into the village from all directions. Still there was no small arms fire from anyone. Only the artillery was spurting out death to the creatures in the jungle.

Harper noticed a man running along a dike parallel to him on his left. It was Minh, and he was trying to catch up with the advance party. Minh was able to make it to a dike that cut right directly across their path of advance. He was out in front of the point man. He was perhaps fifteen meters in front of Harper when a short burst of automatic weapons fire from the edge of the jungle cut him down. There was a surprised look on his face as he fell forward facing Harper…he dropped his rifle and his hands groped at the small of his back. His face hit the water in the paddy and he didn't rise again. The body floated face down.

Firing broke out all along the line of men in the paddy. Everyone was almost submerged in the blackish grimy water. They were receiving fire from two spots along the edge of the jungle. One near the stream bed and one farther to the west of the stream.

Harper grabbed Roan by the arm and shouted at him if he knew enough English to direct the men that he had with him. Roan nodded in agreement.

"Sir, I think that this is only a covering force of perhaps four or five men that will fight a delaying action."

It was Hannaman speaking to Harper.

"Jesus Christ, how am I going to communicate with these people—Roan, you go second platoon and say move left. We will protect them with fire from here. Have number three and four move up behind and go to the right. You understand what I tell you, Roan?" Harper's eyes searched the man, looking for an answer in the confusion of the fight.

"I do, sir."

"Raider six, this is raider forty two. We have contact at the edge of the jungle. Ask forty two Charlie to lay down a base of fire from his position along the stream bed. You acknowledge—over?"

"Four-two, this is six. Roger. I am sending in bravo company to reinforce you now. Can you handle the situation? Over."

"Four-two. Roger...I believe that this is a delaying action by elements in the jungle. Tell forty-two Charlie that he is on target."

Nichols was swooping down on the jungle with the chopper. Both door gunners were blasting away at the jungle area. The men with Harper were still some sixty meters from the edge of the jungle. Slowly his flank elements advanced while they provided a base of fire with the chopper into the area. They advanced leap frogging in this manner.

Harper raised himself from the waters of the paddy and motioned for the men around him to follow him towards the jungle. Slowly the line of men rose and they began to run at a crouch firing from the hip as they went closer to their objective and the men waiting for them in the shadows of the jungle. Paul dropped one of his clips in the water as he was reloading. He didn't stop for it but continued on. The line of men on both sides of him was still with him. A soldier fell to his right, and they continued on.

"Hannaman, call off the ship—we are getting too close." Harper yelled to his friend a few yards away, working both his rifle and the radio on Taylor at the same time.

"Sir, I have bravo six on the horn—he has us in sight and is coming up behind us as fast as possible."

"Right, acknowledge. Tell him to stay in reserve. We may need him as reserve shock force in the jungle if we get into a mess in there."

A roar of screams and yells arose as men began to enter the jungle. The firing continued but it was no longer returned. Harper reached the cover of some palm trees.

"Tell the men to cease fire. Pass it along the line."

There was no one to understand him so he began to motion with his hands—slowly firing died out. Harper went over to his private and took the phone.

"Raider six, this is four-two. So far we have two VC Kia but no weapons." He looked down at the two heaps of flesh which were once living men." I will give you a status report in a few minutes, but we have had light casualties. We lost our two india in the first contact. Over."

"Roger, this is six romeo. I will pass on information to six—he is currently in conference with November Pappas. We have already picked up some suspect. Over. Four-two—roger, out."

"We go to the camp now, Lieutenant?" It was Roan—he had returned to be with Harper. "You take me with you—they do not trust me, and maybe kill."

"No, Roan, but you can go in with our platoon."

Harper looked at the man and wondered if he was afraid of being killed now. Why had he defected in the first place and had volunteered the information? What a strange war. Several men were already dead and perhaps more would die before the morning passed into noon and yet they were going to have a festival in the village to show the natives what good people they really were. But, in actuality, it was a cover-up for the search and the interrogation that would take place and that had already begun with the suspects that they already had. Each side knew what the other was doing and the reasons for it. They had been here before—of that he was positive. Still each side tried to deceive the peasants and the villagers. It was these people who really suffered in the war.

"I know this boy. He worked as a runner from the village to the camp in the past. Troung told him that he would soon be able to join the unit."

"What about the other one, Roan?"

He reached down and rolled the man over. The body was faceless—it had been torn away by a shell.

"Forget it."

Harper repressed the urge to vomit. He

turned and walked away from the bodies. Harper told Taylor to take down the whiplash aerial on the radio as it would just get in the way in the jungle. Besides he made a good target with that thing waving back and forth. Taylor nodded and knelt down to change the antennas.

"Four-two, this is six, I have been trying to contact you. Why haven't you stayed on the radio—over."

"This is four-two. We had some trouble with it, but is corrected now. Over."

"Six. Check out your equipment more closely before you go out next time. I want you to start the advance into the base camp and give me a sit-rep every five minutes. Over."

"Four-two wilco out."

The stream bed went from ankle deep water to waist deep in a few yards as they descended down and into the jungle area itself. There were high stream banks on each side as the men advanced by two into the dim light and the unknown. Each man took a careful and measured step. Everyone strained their ears for the slight indications of the enemy being present and waiting for them around the next bush or the next step. The banks themselves were covered with dense foliage. You could not tell where the bank began—it was easy to lose your foothold if you chose to scale the banks as the weeds and bushes were slippery. That was not the only problem. A man behind Taylor screamed an inhuman sound.

He began to shake and spit black vomit. A long green snake slithered away from the man in the water and into the bank on the other side. Two men took the man out of the jungle and carried him to a chopper that they called for him. But the man was dead before they left the jungle with his tortured body.

After what seemed an endless amount of time they found the approach to the base camp. On one side of the stream there was a bunker covering the approach to the camp, but it was deserted. Smoke arose from the top of the other side of the stream bed. Fires caused by the artillery strike were still burning. Slowly the men climbed the banks of the stream. Here the earth showed recent use on the bank as there was a well-used path leading to the top. The camp looked deserted. There were scattered cooking fires still burning. The logs on one bunker were smoldering. Pieces of clothes and equipment were all over the area. Roan took Harper to the concealed entrance to the tunnel system.

"In here is the hospital and the headquarters for the camp. There are many exits, and I do not know all of them or how to find them."

Harper looked at him, and took his pistol out of his holster and gave it to the man. "Here, take this with you and lead the way into the tunnel. Hannaman, you follow him down and grab one of the other Chieu Hois to go with you. If anything happens, you know what to do to our friend here. Make sure that you are the first one out in case of trouble."

"Yes, sir." Hannaman began to take off his web gear and equipment. He watched the other two men disappear into the tunnel, and he slowly lowered himself in head first with his pistol in one hand and a flashlight in the other.

"Raider six, this is four-two—we are in the camp, and I have sent three men into the tunnel complex. It looks like Charlie has taken off. Over."

"Six roger. I am holding bravo company in reserve—if they hear any shooting, they will come in after you. Over."

"Four-two—roger. I think that they would be used to search the other side of the stream bed. Over."

"Six, I agree; they are on their way out."

"Sir, do you mind if I take the radio off my back for a short while as long as I stay with you?"

"Sure, Taylor, take a break. Want a smoke?" Without waiting for a reply, he gave his radio man a cigarette. They were the only things that weren't wet as he kept them in a metal box. The soldier nodded thanks and was lost in his own thoughts again.

Harper returned to the entrance of the tunnel and called down to his friends. "How's it going in there, Hannaman?"

He didn't get an answer from the men in the tunnel. As he was thinking about this his mind and thoughts were distracted by the men around him. They were methodically searching the entire area around the campsite. He felt more at ease and in less danger. These men knew their job. After all they were all former Viet Cong at one time or another. He leaned against a tree and watched as they probed every bush with their bayonets. Nothing was overlooked. Slowly a pile of personal equipment left by the occupants began to take form in front of him. Harper walked over and examined the contents of the equipment on the ground. A carbine with a broken stock, ammunition, clothes, pots, canvas, cigarettes— all items left by men in a hurry to leave. Some of the things had fresh blood stains on them. His hands got sticky. He wiped them off in the dirt and rubbed them on his pants.

It was at this point he heard the muffled but unmistakable sound of a gunshot. He ran back to the tunnel entrance.

He recognized the voice of Hannaman. It sounded like a voice in a water well. It was flat and distant and there was no echo.

"Paul, they are still in here. We can hear them running ahead of us like rats in a trap."

As he said the word rats, his head popped out of the hole.

"Listen, sarge, have the men get out. We can toss some smoke in. That should suffocate them and if it escapes out the other exists that are supposed to be in the area, we can cover their other escape holes with our troops."

"Yes, sir. My other little buddies are right behind me, and they don't need any coaching to get out of here either."

"Taylor, bring me the phone!"

The soldier jumped up from a kneeling position where he had been adjusting the radio on his back when he had heard the shot.

"Come on, Roan, grab my hand." Hannaman gave him assistance to get out of the tunnel. The slim man popped out of the hole like water under pressure.

"Sarge, explain to Roan what I want done. Have those guys look for smoke and fan out in all directions for thirty to forty meters. Have some of them watch the slope on this side of the stream bed too. Shit, they might have dug all the way down there."

As he was talking, he pulled the pin on a grenade and dropped it in the hole. There was a muffled explosion. Before the dust cleared he tossed in two smoke grenades. They hissed as they detonated and slowly green smoke floated out into the air around them.

"Raider six, this is four-two. Over."

"Six go."

"Four-two, I believe the tunnel is still occupied. We have tossed in smoke. Do you have any tunnel rats at your location. We have tossed in smoke. Do you have and tunnel rats at your location? Over."

"Six, negative. I'll get Ranger zulu and have them send a team by chopper. Have your kilo send us a sit-rep on any items you may have picked up."

"Four-two—roger, out."

"Taylor, make a list of the items we have so far and send it in to the CP."

"Right, sir."

Taylor turned around and walked back over to the pile of equipment.

"Lieutenant, these guys are all excited about something. Look, sir, there is smoke by that bamboo thicket over there."

"Right."

He started running over to the Vietnamese soldiers.

"VC!" He yelled.

They got the message. Two men stepped over to the covered opening that had been concealed and began shooting into it. Burrrrrap-burrrrrrap—the slugs pounded into the dirt and entrance to the tunnel. Above the noise he could hear Nichols broadcasting his appeals for the Viet Cong to surrender. But in this clearing in the jungle under growth that had been hacked away by the enemy, he could not see the chopper. He marveled at the genius of the Viet Cong as a jungle fighter and as an expert in concealment. He shook his head.

"Taylor! Tell six that we have located another entrance to the tunnel."

"Hey, Harper, I hear you guys got quite a find here."

He turned around and saw Luttner coming towards him. Luttner was heavy set with closely cropped black hair. For a man of his size he was quick on his feet. He had a light scar on his nose made by a Korean knife in the last war. He had risen through the ranks and had gotten a commission when this war had broken out. Harper had no real opinion of the man. They weren't friends but they had always gotten along since he had been here.

"Yeah. I thought you would be down at the schoolhouse with the detainees and prisoners."

"The old man figured I should be up here for a while and check out the situation. He wants you to take the Chieu Hoi into the village. I will stay here with Hannaman and my interpreter."

"That's fine by me! Do you want my RTO too?"

"Ah, yeah, you better leave him. I left mine in the village at the CP. They needed two radios back there."

"See you around, Captain."

Luttner walked over to the pile of weapons and equipment. Harper motioned Roan to follow him.

"You leaving, lieutenant?"

Harper nodded his head. "Sorry about that! See you in the village later on, Sarge."

"Sure thing."

Harper decided to take his dead interpreter back to the village himself so that he could be sent back to his relatives in Saigon. When he left the jungle he headed for the rice paddy he believed to hold the man's body. Roan had been lost in his own thoughts and started off in a more direct line to the village. Harper yelled at him and the defector headed back in Harper's direction. Both of them stayed off the dikes and went through the water. There was always the possibility of a sniper in the area. Finally they reached the body. It was still floating face down in the water. The body had tilted to one side and had begun to get hard. Harper had difficulty getting it over his shoulder in a fireman's carry. Finally Roan came to his assistance. The two of them managed to accomplish the task. Roan fished Minh's helmet out of the water and put that on and carried his weapon. The three men headed for the road and to the village.

The morning sun was baking the surface of the earth. As they walked along the road their feet sent up little puffs of dust. The dust blew in their faces from the wind. Harper was sweating from his burden. He put the body down on the road and motioned for Roan to pick up the feet. So the two of them carried their comrade into the village in this manner and placed him in the shade of a well and threw a blanket of canvas over him to shade his eyes from the sun and the rays of light from the day for the last time.

"Is that Sergeant Minh?"

"Yes, major, that's him."

"I am sorry. He was a good man and very reliable. I'll see to it that he gets a full military burial and that his family gets some money to tide them through for a while.

"Thank you, sir."

Lancaster asked Harper to go over to the school and monitor the interrogation team and see what information they could come up with. He was to take Roan with him and stop on the way to pick up his girlfriend.

As they walked through the village, they could see that the festival had begun in the town. All of the people had been gathered in the village square. There were long lines of people going into tents for various activities. There were movies for the children and doctors for the sick and aged. Dentists pulled teeth as the only solution for teeth problems. Others were queued in line for parcels of food and clothing being given out. Conspicuous was the absence of the men.

Harper walked into a small hut on the edge of the town and there he met Tuy Von. Her father was gone. She alone waited for the outcome of the last few days with the stoic composure of the oriental. For a peasant girl she was very beautiful. Her teeth were white because she didn't chew beetle nut. Her long black hair fell to her shoulders. The face was highlighted by eyes that were dark and mysterious. They smiled at you and told you nothing. She was in short intriguing.

"She be my wife," Roan said with a smile.

"That's fine, Roan, that is fine. Is she ready to go with us now?"

The two of them spoke for a moment. Harper walked outside. He felt they needed the privacy of a few moments, something which they may not have for days to come while they were kept in the Chieu Hoi center with many, many others like them.

The two of them left the hut holding hands.

She carried a small wicker bag with her clothes in it and some cooking utensils.

"She ready, sir. She say good-bye to father already. He has gone, and she does not know where.

There was a broken ox cart wheel in the front yard as they left the house. Someone had worked on it recently. It lay there unfinished. The roof was sagging on one corner of the hut. It too needed repairs. There were no animals in the yard. The house had a deserted look already. One of many in a long war.

Chapter Eleven
Dorothy

The days and nights had become routine. There were many villages to search. Occasionally, at night, their camp was attacked by the Viet Cong and they in turn were always repulsed. A few men were killed and wounded and others succumbed to various tropical diseases. Dysentery was always a problem. Finally a man could work out an arrangement with the ailment, and that was diarrhea three times a day like clockwork. If you didn't go run down, you could live with the problem.

Harper had become restless, and it began to show up in his work. It was actually a common malady for all of the men in this country. You began to take too many chances for no apparent reason. Life became cheap and had little meaning. Mail from home started to lose its meaning because the writers had no idea of what these men faced every day of their lives and sleepless nights. Death grew like a fear of cancer. It stalked everyone everywhere.

Finally the soul said the hell with it. If it came—it came. And there was nothing that a mortal could do about it.

The Christmas holidays were approaching. This meant some type of a truce. The men could get leave in country. Harper chose to go to Saigon and see Dorothy. With a clean pair of uniforms and a pistol under his belt, he took a hop on the first chopper to Tan San Nhut Air Base in Saigon.

Like a salmon returning home to spawn he headed for Dorothy's apartment and three days of rest and comfort.

The crowds in the streets were still the same; they never changed. Humanity bumped and bustled beside each other for survival in a ravaged land. All faces looked the same. They had a dead earnestness in their outward appearance. Every man acted like a shark to get the better of his neighbor, and the neighbor believed the world was made up of fish in the sea. All one had to do is to catch a fish and put it on the table for sacrificial rites.

The hallway to the apartment was dim and lacked lighting. He approached the door. As he did so, his stomach began to turn. Perhaps she was not there or even worse she might have another visitor. She had sent him a note a few days before. It contained a twenty dollar bill and an invitation to join her for the holiday. He had forgotten that Benjeman had left the money on the table. So he had returned it to the man just yesterday at his office. He knocked but there was no answer from inside.

The door handle was ajar and he opened the door and went inside the apartment.

A lump came to his throat. In one corner of the living room there was a Christmas tree. Outside the heat was 105 degrees. But the tree gave the room a cooler appearance. He walked over to it and noticed that there were some presents addressed to him and all wrapped in beautiful paper. Harper decided to go down and find some gifts for her on the black market.

He did not have to go far to find one of the thousands of vendors of black market goods on the streets. They were in front of the hotel and extended for blocks on the streets in all directions. He went to a stand that had a large array of goods from the main PX which was on the other side of the city. It would save him the cab fare and a wait in lines which would produce nothing when he got there because they would be out of the items in the first place.

It was in fact a small department store and had all that he could want to buy in one single location. As he went through the items he finally chose some French perfume that was nicely boxed. Just as he was about to leave he noticed a small pearl necklace that still had the PX price tag on it. He offered ten dollars less than the tag and the woman sold it. With these gifts under his arm he continued down the street to find something for Joyce too. In another stall on the sidewalk, he discovered some cashmere sweaters. Harper bought two of them, a yellow one for Joyce and a lavender for Dorothy. Thus armed he went back to the apartment. He stopped in the liquor store on the main floor and bought two bottles of champagne to celebrate Christmas Eve with the two of them.

When he returned upstairs he found Joyce in the apartment. She invited him in and informed him that Dorothy would return from a hospital visit in a few minutes. He sat down on the couch and she brought him a cold beer from the kitchen.

"Paul, you are going to have to excuse me for a few minutes—I have a date tonight and I must take a shower and get ready. Please make yourself at home."

"Thanks and I will."

He listened as the shower water began running in the bathroom. He thought about the time that he and Benjeman had been here together and how many times had he thought about it before today. On lonely nights in the field and during the day on some strange road going he knew not where. In this land of emotion this was an island of refuge from the storm that surrounded it. He was safe in this apartment.

He wondered why Joyce had not asked about the presents that he had brought with him. Perhaps she felt that she would not be included and thought better not to say anything. Paul got up and placed them all under the tree. He bent down and turned on the lights. They were multi-colored and blinked slowly on and off. They had done a nice job with the tree he thought to himself. His legs swung up on the couch and he fell asleep waiting for Dorothy to return.

"Darling, you were so sweet to think of me and bring the presents." He felt her soft hands on his chest. The scent of her body was all around him. Dorothy was sitting on the edge of the couch. Her hands caressed his forehead and gently slid along his chest.

Paul sat up and took her in his arms. There was no need to say anything. They both understood the feelings of the other. Words were only a hindrance and needed for those that feel the need for additional security. Their bodies and their desire told them all that they needed to know.

Paul took her by the hand and led her into the bedroom. Once again the neighbors were having a party. Only this time it was Christmas music that could be heard filtering in through the window. Dorothy helped his fumbling hands undress her. Piece by piece her lovely skin came into view in the soft light of the sun reflecting through the window.

Their bodies yielded to one another with passion and fire in the heat of the day. When it was over they lay stretched on the bed together naked. She was now to become his confessor. To her he could tell his innermost thoughts and ideas.

Paul dropped his hand over the edge of the bed and picked up his shirt off the floor. He reached in the pocket and pulled out a pack of cigarettes and offered her one as he placed one in his mouth.

"I am sick of the war. I have lost my individuality, and life means nothing to me anymore."

"Darling, you can't mean that. I have lived every day with the sick and wounded that are returning from the field. The Viet Cong are controlled by the Communists. We are fighting a war against the corruption of the communists over the people. Look at the way our people are suffering and taking the brunt of the fighting. It must be right. You can't really mean what you say."

"Dorothy, I can't mean anything any more. Have you ever witnessed the dead being dragged out of a tunnel? I killed those men a few weeks ago. We suffocated them to death. Their faces had turned blue, their eyes bulged; and their tongues hung out of their mouths. What is it all for? I keep losing friends in the fields. Their young lives are lost for nothing. The politicians on both sides keep talking of peace and bombing halts and yet nothing is accomplished but the continual and grizzly slaughter of men on both sides. You should see the interrogation rooms that we civilized soldiers set up to torment our prisoners. Granted I am sure that they treat the people that they get the same way. But of what use is it. What do these small villages and hills and jungles mean to men that they can't stop the fighting and come to the peace table. The beatings, the torture, and murder—I can't stop having nightmares about it. Some people that I have been in contact with have literally lost their sanity already. Our enemies are in no position to storm the beaches of our country. We are the aggressors. The peasants want peace in the countryside. They don't care who wins. Our government agencies aid and abet the corruption in this country. It is no wonder that the people rebel from foreign intervention. We have no more right in this country than the North Vietnamese. And at least they, they have a cultural heritage! Did I ever mention Sergeant Lord to you? Well he is married and has several children back in the States. Do you know that he will never be with them again. Not because he is dead but because one night on patrol he got scared and shot what he thought to be a VC. This guy was a villager returning home from the field where he had been working late building a water well for irrigation. Sergeant Lord will spend the rest of his life in prison. They want us to fight a war and then they tie our hands behind us and crucify us if we make a mistake. There is no justice anymore. No one can make me believe otherwise.

"You should see some of the propaganda that we have picked up off of the dead Viet Cong. They are filled with the unrest of our own society. And yet we, like the French, Japanese, and Chinese, are trying to force our culture, our methods, and our war down their throats. Do you know how many people this government in Saigon represents in the countryside. Practically none. Why? Because they don't have the allegiance of the people. They need us to take them out to the grass roots level and tell the people what good they are doing. They need our guns and tanks to do a job where they should be able to walk freely among their own people. But the country is ruled by the Viet Cong. Sure, they use terror and murder but no more than what I have witnessed our allies do in the name of democracy.

"When we talk to the villagers they all remember the Emperor and the old feudal system with a great deal of fondness. Now how can we erase this from their minds? They gave their allegiance to one man who was their feudal lord, and he in turn protected them. At least they had a government structure. Today they have nothing. If they want anything done they must pay the government many times what it is worth through corruption. The Viet Cong extract taxes and do not have the physical means to accomplish great projects. Where would your loyalty be in a situation like this? They live in fields of despair. They have no where to turn for help. The populace is caught in the middle."

"Come on, Paul, you are just distressed because the holidays are here and you are not home. I can understand what you feel but you should not go around telling people what you just told me. You could end up court-martialed. You would not make a great martyr, darling, because no one is going to believe you."

Paul felt much better to let off the suppression of his thoughts to someone he could trust. He did not answer her directly. He reached over and kissed her on the lips and placed his hand on her stomach. She giggled and threw the sheets over them both.

They had dinner in the apartment. Instead of the usual turkey and dressing for the meal they had broiled steak—something which was more of a rarity in the field than turkey. The two of them ate in relative silence. Both were perhaps doing some reflecting on their recent conversation.

For their first night together they decided to go out on the town and take in some of the local nightclubs. Most of the better ones were in walking distance of the apartment. As they reached the outdoors they were greeted by a cool breeze from the south, something which was a rarity in this country. The only difference in the city at night was simply that it was night and perhaps more dangerous to be on the streets. The black markets were still operating in full force. They were doing a land office business with last minute Christmas shoppers. Most shoppers were buying presents-for girl or boyfriends, as gifts for families back in the states had been sent home weeks before, so that they could arrive there in time for the rush Christmas mails.

The Carevelle Hotel was a relatively new establishment that had been built from graft and corruption. It was lavish and expensive and it had good entertainment. So it was their first stop. As they entered the show bar, Harper recognized a face at a table. It was Lancaster. Both of the men seemed to see each other at the same time and there was no way to avoid each other's company.

"Well, Paul, would you and your lady friend care to join me. As you can see I am a loner tonight."

"Sir, this is Dorothy Goddard. I guess we can join you for a short time. We were expecting her roommate to arrive and the four of us were going to the Brinx Hotel later on. We understand that they have a good band from the Philippines tonight. Perhaps, if you aren't doing anything, you would like to join us."

"I appreciate the invitation, but I think that another hot shower in the hotel and getting into the sack early tonight is what I need more than anything else."

The three of them sat there exchanging uncomfortable glances at one another for a few minutes. A waiter arrived, and they ordered some drinks. The situation was eased when the band began to blare out some music which made conversation all but impossible. Finally, the major rose and said goodnight and left for his shower.

As the tempo of the band slowed down its pace of music, they got up from the table and began to dance. She was wearing a loose sheath dress with a low cut front. Her body felt good next to his as they swayed back and forth to the rhythm of the band. Overhead were multi-colored lights that revolved above the dance floor and changed the lighting effect every few seconds. Gradually they were able to make their way over to the outdoor balcony. As they danced here, they had a beautiful view of the city at night. Cabs, busses, and bikes whirled by below them in a stream of light and noise. There was still a cool breeze from the south and it made the tightly packed dance floor more bearable. When they returned to their table there were fresh drinks waiting for them. At least they had a thoughtful waiter. He was one of those relics from the history of the country. He was French and in all probability a leftover from the days of the French rule. He undoubtedly stayed on with a native wife and family. There were many of these types scattered around the country, not to mention large sections of Chinese and Indians with their tailor shops and restaurants.

Since they had not actually planned on waiting for Joyce in the club and they didn't care to run into any more people that they might know, they went back to the apartment. It was hot and stuffy inside. They turned on the ceiling fans that hung in the center of each room They brought some relief and cool air from the outside.

The two of them sat down together facing the Christmas tree. Like thousands on this night they decided to open the presents before morning. She gave Paul a shirt and a pair of sport pants and a tie to match. She enjoyed her presents also. After the initial excitement of opening the gifts and presents they had little to say to each other and gazed into the lights on the tree as if it were a fireplace somewhere back in the States where life was more normal than here.

"Paul, I have been thinking over about some of the things that you have told me. I want you to know that you worry me quite a bit. It seems to me that your ideas contradict themselves. First you are for the war and then you are against it entirely. It must be confusing out there in the field with all of the personal losses that you must suffer day after day with little or no thanks at the end—except perhaps some ribbon that says you have been a good boy, like something you might get in the boy scouts."

"You don't understand what I have told you. All that I have said comes out of me in part because of my involvement and indoctrination by the army; but it is my moral selfhood that rebels to the entire idea of this war and what it actually stands for and as to what it is accomplishing. Can't you see that no matter what the outcome and no matter who is going to win, everyone like you and I are the losers—we can do nothing. Power does not belong to us nor to the people who we are supposed to be fighting for in the first place. This war is history just repeating itself again. I really believe that this conflict is no different and no better than the Spanish Civil war of the 1930s. Each side is testing weapons and methods and techniques, and you and I and all those who are dying are just the victims of power politics. It is a crime that man in his quest for good—that he has left so few with the power and destiny over the lives of so many. The crime is that the masses on the whole believe all the garbage that their leaders spurt out at them like puss from a wound."

"Paul, what has gotten into you out there that you can think this way." Her face had a look of bewilderment and disbelief. She could not believe the words that this man was telling her.

"I'll tell you what is bothering me. I am sick of killing and seeing faces of death at every step that I take. I have a whole life ahead of me, and no government has the right to say where my life is going to cease to exist just because I was born there or because I have some obligation to a society because it is my duty. Duty is a dirty word. It can mean murder and rape and destruction. What makes us any different. Not a god damn thing. I see facts and statistics about areas that we have pacified and that have come under government control. That is all bullshit. We could not even get to one of those places tonight without being killed on the way or murdered in our beds after we got there. Lies! The whole damn war is nothing but mountains of lies made and remade by both sides."

Before she had a chance to answer, Joyce returned without her date. She looked rather depressed. When they inquired what had happened it seems as though she ran into another fellow who had asked her out and the two men had gotten into a quarrel which the MP's had broken up. The outcome being she was left without a date and the police gave her a ride home. Paul was able to brighten her spirits with the present that he brought for her.

Once in the bedroom again, they had no differences, only flesh against flesh and body against body in an age old rhythm that was endless and that formed the seeds of life.

Chapter Twelve
A Bend in the Road

Troung sat in the coffee shop in the village of Ben Cat having his morning breakfast. He watched as the US convoys went up and down the road of route thirteen and over the one bridge that linked it to the town from the North. From where he sat he could observe the traffic coming in both directions. Although he was planning another mission his mind was musing over the recent losses in this life. In a few days it would be the national TET festival and another truce. Over the past few months he had lost his wife, and one of his trusted friends had defected to the other side. He still seethed within himself, with rage, over Roan's betrayal. There were many courses of action left open to him to get even with both the government and Roan. But first he had to locate the traitor and then deal with him publicly in a village square to serve as an example.

On this particular morning, however, he had other things, about which to think. There was an American civilian from the province center who worked with the refugees in this area as of late. He was going to get this man. He looked down at his watch. It was 8:10. The jeep came into view as it speeded north, over the bridge, and to the camp on the other side. There were always two or three men in the vehicle, and they were not well armed. They had the fat, complacent look of American conquerors, he thought to himself. This would not be the ambush site as it was too near the center of the village and too close to the national police post. But he could get at them only a few yards from their own camp at a bend in the road. He had been there every morning or at some time during the day selling ice to the Americans. Now it was only a question of the right moment and the precise second to spring the trap.

Troung began to reflect on his past and his years with the resistance. He had joined the Viet Cong because his father had been an officer in the Viet Minh. He came from a peasant family, and they had always had nothing but peasantry. They watched as the rich landlords got the pick of the lands and taxed the peasants until they could pay no more. Then the French had come and nothing had changed for the life of those who must live off the land for existence. They, the French, promised much and provided little but their promises. Then again the Americans came first indirectly with the government that they supported in Saigon. Gradually they began to send more supplies, more guns to support dictators, and finally, when all else was lost and exhausted, men and then more men, then divisions of soldiers to support a handful of corruption. The Americans promised many things, and the more they promised and built for their own necessity, and for show, the more the corruption grew and the more the peasants suffered. Thus he felt himself a true liberator of his country. He had a mission; and he would carry it out if it meant his death and the death of all of those who followed with him.

Troung noticed Hinh on his bike on the road, weaving through the traffic and coming in his direction. This was the last of his trusted friends. Now he could not be sure if he could trust anyone. All of his young boys had died men in the jungle and along the sides of roads as they fought from ambush. Some died in a tunnel because they were not able to escape with the rest of them down to the exit on the river bed. Traitors, deserters, and the dead; that was all that could fill his memory. His wife too. She also had died and for nothing. At least he had killed the district chief Tinh many weeks before. He wondered when the land would finally be free and he could seek out a new wife and start a family in a free land, a land without fear of war and bombs by day and attacks by night. Then he smiled inwardly to himself because he too was a part of the total picture. His motives and his ideals had caught him like a fish in a net and there was no turning back to the past. There could only be the future; and for it he must fight and run and live to fight again.

A large convoy moved by the restaurant, and a huge cloud of dust settled over the inhabitants of the area. Everything had red dirt clinging to it. It was something that neither man nor machine could completely erase from the body that encased them.

"Is the ice ready at the store yet?"

"Yes, we can go down on my bike and pick it up. It is going to be a hot day. This should be good for business."

"Let us waste no time then. Let's go."

The compound was relatively small. It originally had served to house some thirty Vietnamese soldiers and their families. Now it was used as a halfway house for American convoys and other travelers in the area. There was now a permanent contingent of American advisors living here, and they had, with typical American industrious, erected a beautiful bar for thirsty travelers. All you needed was your money.

There were, however, certain disadvantages of living in this particular compound. It smelled. Rather it was rank. There were two latrines that had been used for years and had never been disinfected. The Americans built their own and took care of it but this did not solve the problem of their allies. Then, of course, there were pigs and goats roaming the yards of the enclosure. Each has a distinct stench all to its own, not to mention that there was a war going on outside this compound which only served to make the entire situation less than bearable.

Major Randolph Clay was the officer in charge of the American side of the camp. He was from Savannah, Georgia. He had definite likes and dislikes. To bring this point home the first thing he did was to post guards between his part of the camp and the Vietnamese. This accomplished he then set out to build a barbed wire barrier across the camp completely cutting off the Vietnamese from access to his side of the wire. It was all part of his belief in separate but equal facilities. It was believed that if he had been assigned any Negro soldiers, they too could have joined the Vietnamese as personal advisors to maintain a close allied relationship on the Vietnamese side of the wire. Major Clay was also a drunkard which served to make the days pass more easily for him and his men. He was rather happy-go-lucky and had a devil-may-care attitude because, after all, they would only be here for one year and anyone could survive that with a good book and a bottle of gin or whatever else was available.

The help in the kitchen was always busy preparing food of one type or another. This was done because of the major's orders. There was a huge fan that pushed the cooking smoke out of the kitchen into the major's room where he had a fan in the window and brought the odors into his room. This would usually cut off the other less desirable smells in the area from reaching his sensitive nostrils. The food could be sold to passing soldiers. So while he made money he also solved the odor problem in his section of the camp.

The men and officers slowly began to form the habits of the major. There was a constant stream of traffic, of the women from the village in and out of the quarters of the men. They came and left at all hours of the day and night. The men were rowdy and dressed casually in both civilian and military clothes. The cook had a pair of Viet Cong black fatigues tailor-made for himself and he spent the day walking around in these things. Bermudas and a steel helmet were popular. A T-shirt and a helmet were even more popular. Because of his position of authority, the major was usually found in his boots. He was one of the few that wore them around the camp.

On this particular day the men grumbled as usual because they didn't receive enough ice from the village and that what they got was not enough to quench all of their thirsts. They didn't trust the two ice men at all, perhaps because they were both of military age and were not in the army. Of course many Vietnamese took a second job out of the military and catered to the needs of the Americans… women, beer, food, gifts, laundry, and ice. But, of course, they had no real reason not to trust the men so they were always invited into the camp for a morning beer and a couple of American cigarettes.

The sun rose in the sky and baked earth and

man as the day progressed from dawn to dusk. The men had erected a tennis court, but it was only used in the cool of the evening. The doctor in the camp had little to do except treat the girls with penicillin shots to protect the men. But once in a while he missed one and one of the men had to place his manhood on ice for a few days and sustain from alcohol and women. But this did not faze the men at all. There was nothing else to do. They were all here as advisors and their Vietnamese troops chose not to do anything either. After all a man could get killed going out on patrols. The local Viet Cong gave the camp a wide birth and left them alone. It was an unwritten agreement between the two sides to leave well enough alone. Let others fight the war and die. So really the Americans had no one to advise except themselves. All three parties were in agreement not to upset the apple cart. There were other places like this in the country such as Vung Tau and Nha Trang. These were rest centers for the troops of both sides. The war swirled around them both and it did not enter these areas. Ben Cat was just a magnification of this on a small scale. There were occasional incidents. Once in a while the Viet Cong would fire one or two mortar shells into the compound just to let the defenders know that they were still out there and sometimes the Viet Cong would ambush some local Vietnamese for some personal grudge, like the man did not pay his taxes. Other than that, it was hard to tell that a war was going on in this area. For these troops and others like them around the country, the war was something that they watched on the local television at night or read in the Stars and Stripes. But this was only two days before TET and then perhaps history would soon write a different story.

Benjeman parked his jeep in the shade of a tree. He was very proud of himself. He had been able to locate the supplies to feed and house all of these people and had got enough to make a little money on the side for himself. His eyes surveyed the refugees' camp. It was rather typical of most of these temporary camps. There were Red Cross tents set up for families but they were not adequate simply because the heat made them uninhabitable. Some families had found tin and boards and were able to erect makeshift hovels to place their families and their belongings. The children were one of the biggest headaches, with which to contend. They were all over and in everyone's hair at the same time. They would steal anything on which they could get their hands. They would surround you in droves. A man did not have a chance if he had anything of value on him or his jeep. Benjeman had managed to get hold of some soccer balls at the USO in Di An, and these seemed to occupy their time, at least for a while.

He rather enjoyed living with Major Clay simply because the man did not interfere with his work or get in his way. He had become a good friend of the local police chief in a short period of time. They had much in common, these two men—mostly the love of money. He had been trading food and supplies for more weapons which he could then sell on the black market in Saigon. This temporary assignment had been a boom to his finances. He could and would be a very rich man in a short period of time.

The only thing that he really missed was his secretaries. The local girls in the village were not to his liking. The nicest one belonged to the police chief, and he was not about to give her up; not even for money. So in this respect Benjeman felt hindered in this small backwater village which was out of the main stream of what he considered Vietnamese life.

Troung and Hinh were sitting in the yard of the compound enjoying the last few puffs on an American smoke. This had become part of the routine to gain the confidence and trust of the Americans. On some occasions, they would bring some local beer with them or native rice wine. Thus armed it did not take long for the Americans to accept them as friends. Granted doubt still persisted in the minds of some, but on the whole they both had access to the camp without any problems. Soon the doctor would have his hands full because of the trust placed in these men.

The next morning began like any other except that Troung was not at his usual place for breakfast. He was down by the river at the ice plant with Hinh. All night they had been breaking soda pop bottles into fine pieces of glass and pouring this lethal weapon into the molds where the ice was being manufactured. It was the day before the TET holiday and the truce period for the entire country. The roads were heavy with holiday traffic as soldiers of both sides began long journeys to their family homes. Ox carts, bicycles, scooters, and cars filled the roads. It was a mass exodus from a year of strife and turmoil. All were happy and at ease save a few select units of the Viet Cong. Their mission was to regroup in cities throughout the country and hit the government posts and offices and destroy the government's hold on the people. Weapons had been smuggled into towns through the use of funeral processions for weeks before the big offensive.

The two of them headed for the compound with their load of ice. It glistened in the morning sun. It looked pure and clean and cold. They came to a bend in the road before the entrance to the camp. The vegetation along the sides of this stretch of land came up to the road bend, and you could not see the camp from this location. Along both sides of it now were Troung's men. They had slowly been infiltrating into the area for the past two days. Now they lay in wait for the effect of the ice to take hold on the men in the compound. Troung could feel his men's presence as they went past but he gave no sign of recognition. He could feel their eyes on him.

The guards of the camp waved the two men in a usual without bothering to check them for weapons. Of course they never would have to carry their weapon on a mission such as this one. Death and pain would arrive this time unexpectedly in the camouflage of something which they used every day. It would be like walking out the front door in the morning to get the paper and have it explode in your face.

Troung accepted the money for the ice and began repeating the word TET several times to let it be known that he and his friend had business elsewhere this morning and could not wait for the usual beer and cigarettes.

The men in the camp wished them good-bye and took the ice to the mess hall for use in the morning juice. The cook placed the ice in some sawdust and began chopping off some pieces to place in everyone's glass for the orange juice.

Charlie was a mongrel dog which lived in and around the kitchen and served as the camp mascot. It was the dog and not one of the men who discovered the glass first. Peters the cook usually gave the dog a piece of ice to chew on because the dog enjoyed it. This morning was no exception. It wasn't long before one of the men noticed the dog bleeding from the mouth. It began whimpering on the floor. Blood was streaming out of its mouth. One of the privates asked the cook if he had broken anything on the floor lately. When the cook said no they immediately sent for the doctor. It did not take long for the doctor to find a jagged piece of glass stuck in the dog's mouth. The cook took a large piece of ice and placed it in the sink and poured hot water on it. Finally they found the evidence, for which that they had been waiting. A few pieces of glass lay on the bottom of the sink.

By this time, Major Clay had arrived for breakfast and had noticed the commotion in the kitchen. When he heard the news, he sobered up immediately. He had the men throw out all food bought on the local market. This included bread, vegetables, fruit, and some meat. He called for an immediate conference in the kitchen of all officers. Slowly they began to arrive. Some were still not dressed and had been awakened for the meeting.

"Gentlemen, the Viet Cong have sabotaged our food, and this leads me to believe that we may possibly be facing an attack. Alert the Division in the rear and inform them of the situation and to stand by. We are going to send out a patrol into the jungle area north of our position. I want the patrol to circle two hundred meters to the east before they enter the area. Take one platoon of the Vietnamese and six of our own men. I will lead one company of men up the road to the bend and wait for you there. From this position, we can cover both sides of the road to block any escape. Hamilton, you take one man and two squads and enter the jungle from the west and head for the road. Stay in constant radio contact with me. I shall wait until you both are in position before we move up the road. Now, get your gear and start moving."

Major Clay personally went past the wire to the other side of the camp. He went to see the commander of the Vietnamese as he was having his morning meal with his family. Through an interpreter he made the man understand the situation. He too reacted immediately. Soon men were running out of their barracks in battle gear and ready for what was to come.

At this point, Major Clay remembered that the civilian would be going down that road to the refugee camp shortly. He ran back to his compound to warn the man not to leave the camp until the area was cleared. As they were talking, Major Clay thought that perhaps it would be a clever idea if he used Benjeman's jeep to scout out front with his troops following closely behind. If there was to be an ambush on the road, he would be the decoy and the Viet Cong would be caught in a trap before they knew what had happened.

Troung looked at his watch. The jeep with the American should be coming down the road shortly. They had hidden the bike in the foliage along the road. It would be a perfect ambush. If the men from the compound came out to rescue these people, they would be caught in a cross fire on the road. Hinh was waiting on the other side with his men. They had built up strength to some fifty-three men again. Most of them were young boys with the revolutionary spirit. They needed a quick and easy victory to boost their morale. He felt sure that the men in the camp would now be bleeding from the glass. This would then prevent any help from reaching the men in the jeep they were going to ambush. Again he looked down at his watch and wondered why the jeep had not shown up yet. He heard the noise of an engine; he flicked his weapon off the safety switch. He relaxed again as it was a local bus going into the village. It was jammed with holiday travelers. One man was riding on the rear bumper of the bus. Chickens were sticking out windows, and the squeal of small pigs could be heard as they went on their last journey to the holiday tables.

Troung had found himself in positions like this many times before but he began to feel more uneasy than usual. The jeep was late. It had happened before but they were so close to the camp. Perhaps something had gone wrong. He began to worry about the operation. He was almost on the verge of calling it off when he once again heard the sound of an engine coming up the road from the direction of the camp.

It was the USAID jeep. He got ready to fire. He heard the rustle of branches coming from behind him and thought nothing of it. Perhaps one of his men had gone to relieve himself in the bushes and was returning to his position. This was his first and last fatal mistake. He aimed his rifle and began to fire. His bullets were kicking up clouds of dirt along the road. Firing began all around him. It was too fast and too much to be that of his men alone. The occupants jumped from the jeep and rolled into a ditch along the side of the road. Firing got louder on his right rear. He rolled to his left and jumped to a sitting position. Troops.

Troops were all around them. They were coming from their rear in the jungle. He yelled for the men to make a break for the road and head for the other side. He began running and turning and firing his weapon at his adversaries. He reached the road and made a dash for the jungle on the other side. Bullets hit the ground near him and came from both sides of the road. He fell, Troung dropped his rifle and began to moan. He crawled in the dirt searching for the gun but the blood in his face would not let his eyes find anything. Slowly the realization came to him that he was blind. He screamed and held his hands to his face; where his eyes and nose should have been there was nothing.

Slowly the firing died down around him. He lay on the road not knowing if he was facing the earth or the sky. The pain was beginning to become unbearable. He felt a boot standing on his hand. He must have been close to his weapon. A strange voice said, "This one is blind. He is one of the lucky ones."

Troung could not see the slaughter of his men. They laid where they fell. They were dressed in black and in shorts and without shoes. Some leered, some stared into nothing, but most of all were dead. He felt cold hands lift his body into a truck. There was someone tending his wounds, but the war was over. His life was over. The world of color and sights and smells were gone. His mission was over.

Chapter Thirteen
Beginnings And Endings

All that Harper could ascertain from the briefing was that all hell had broken loose up and down the countryside. They had been rushed into the Province center to put down some Viet Cong that had taken refuge in the marketplace. They were in the center of town along the river front. Some of the men had been doing some house to house fighting. There were still some occasional shots heard. At the present time, they were in a blocking position to keep the enemy from escaping into the river. His group was holding the local post office in Phy Coung. The fighting was going on presently about two blocks from their position. Some of their group had been rushed to Saigon and other areas. This had been the first time that the Viet Cong had actually made an attack during their own truce and national holiday.

He was thinking about some of the other men. Nichols had finally made it home safely. He had left two weeks ago. Hannaman was in the hospital with malaria and he had been planning on paying him a visit that afternoon, but now he was in the middle of the war again. Dorothy was going to have a baby, and he had not had a chance to get to see her and ask her to marry him. He had thought that he could make the trip the next morning because of the truce. He did love this girl he had met in this country, although he had not really given marriage a serious thought until he had received her letter just two days before. She had been wonderful about the whole thing and she certainly was not pressuring him about marriage. So he had given it some thought and he really didn't know anyone else that he liked any better than her. Besides she was one of the first women to whom he could talk, and felt that she understood him to some extent.

Farther on down the street and in a house that was pockmarked by bullets a man was standing in the shadow of a doorway. He was talking to a young boy about eleven years old. The man had a rifle slung across his shoulder. There was a box in his hand. It was about the size of three cigarette packs. He was offering the boy twenty cents if he would take the package to the Americans and give it to one of the men as a gift. Finally the boy accepted and he ran out on the street to join some refugees from some of the buildings that were burning a few yards away.

Harper was on the radio speaking to Luttner. Luttner was leading some of the assault troops against the Viet Cong positions. Someone yelled that there were some refugees on the street. He told a sergeant to get on the street and search them for weapons. Then he continued his conversation with Luttner. The radio was on the floor of the building. Taylor was standing guard at the door.

The room was vacant except for a broken table in one corner. There was blood on the wall made there recently. Perhaps the Viet Cong had passed through here with their wounded before they got there.

"Sir, the sergeant says that there is some kid out here without any family. He wants to know what you want him to do with the kid."

Harper wasn't listening to Taylor. He had the earphones on and was still conversing with Luttner. A slender figure appeared in the doorway. A small hand produced a little box and dropped in on the floor. The child turned and ran. Taylor yelled, "Hey!" Those were his last words. The shrapnel from the grenade tore into his body. He was jolted against the doorway and slid to the ground in a sitting position; then his body rolled over and fell halfway into the sidewalk.

The explosion had knocked the radio phone out of Harper's hands. He bent down to call in a medical evacuation ship for Taylor. The radio was dead. He went over to Taylor and bent down to look at the man. He noticed that his own pants were wet. He began to feel a sharp pain. It slowly became worse and worse. He began to cry. This was his blood. Taylor was beyond help at this point. Soldiers were all around them. He remembered seeing a small boy lying on the street—his neck was severed from his body. He wondered how the boy got involved in this. Overhead he heard the drone of a chopper. This time it was for him. He was getting dizzy. The world began to turn round and round. He blacked out. He remembered no more. His memory was blank.

When his eyes opened again, he felt a needle in his arm or rather he could see it there. There were lights in the ceiling above him. He could see the white masks on the men surrounding him. He heard the words pulse...morphine...scalpel...suture...and then he blacked out once again.

Slowly the effect of the drugs and the operation began to wear off of him. He began to have periods of consciousness. His mind started to recall where he had been and what had happened. Finally he was able to ask a nurse about Taylor. Where was he? Why wasn't he in the next bed to him? She replied that she didn't know a Taylor, but that she would inquire for him. Once again the pain became too much to bear and he asked for another shot. The doctor said that he had enough already. He could not give him any more unless it was absolutely necessary. His whole body ached with pain and discomfort. His arm was in a cast. But most of the pain came from his stomach.

Three doctors were in conference in a small office at the end of the ward. They were discussing the case of Lieutenant Paul Harper. They had finally reached agreement that he should be told shortly that he had lost his genitals. A man should know this sort of thing as soon as he is able to take the news without any ill effects to his present condition. The doctors decided which one of them would have the terrible job of bearing the news to him and then they waited to see how his condition improved.

Gradually and day by day, Harper began to feel a little better. He wondered why his voice sounded so different when he spoke to anyone. It sounded a little higher to him than when it was before. He asked the nurses when he could begin to have regular food. The intravenous feeding began to bother him and he did not like having the needles in his arm all the time.

Finally one morning the doctor brought a tray of food to him for breakfast. "Well, Lieutenant, how are you feeling now? You have shown us a lot of improvement these past few days. We believe that you are ready for the trip home and back to the states. In fact you are scheduled to leave the first thing tomorrow."

"God, that is wonderful sir, just wonderful."

"Son," he said placing his hand on Harper's arm, "there is something that you must know before you leave here. You gave us a lot of worry, but as you can see you are going to be fine in the end. There is, however, something that I must tell you. You will not be able to have children."

Harper screamed, "God, no no no, God no." His eyes filled with tears and he began to sob.

It was 5:30 in the morning. Oxen were leading their masters into the rice field below. They followed the age-old traditions of those before them as they went to plow the fields. Children laughed in the villages and mothers and daughters began putting tobacco and rice in the sun to dry and make ready for use. They shielded their eyes from the sun to see a plane pass over. The countryside was dotted by fields of barbed wire put there by man. The wire cut and separated man from man and brother from brother. In the peasant land it served as a reminder that all who live here reside in fields of despair.

A huge jet plane had taken off into the sky carrying its burden of crippled and maimed and dying to perhaps something better at the end of the clouds. As it left the runway and bounds of earth, another plane landed, bringing with it fresh troops and new blood. Harper stopped looking out of the window—he turned over and moaned.

Glossary

AK-47—An automatic assault rifle used by North Vietnamese Vietcong troops.

AO/TAO—The area of operation or tactical area of operation. Defined by both geographic boundaries and "Rules of Engagement."

ARVN—A South Vietnamese soldier. The Army of the Republic of Vietnam.

B-40—Small unit designation used by the Vietcong for a platoon or company sized unit of some 30-120 soldiers. This unit was part of a larger unit operating under the banner of "The Phu Loi Battalion."

BAR—Browning Automatic Rifle.

BAR GIRL—Vietnamese Prostitute.

BODY COUNT—The number of enemy killed (KIA), wounded (WIA), or captured during an operation. These figures were used by the military, Saigon, and Washington to justify men and materials as they were fed into the war machine. The world press became less friendly and more cautious after the 1968 Tet Offensive. They no longer believed the Military figures. This exodus was led by Walter Cronkite at CBS. Tet lead to the eventual American withdrawal from the war.

C AND C—The Command and Control aircraft that circled overhead to direct the combined air and ground operations.

CHICOM—Chinese Communist. Also an assault rifle.

CHIEU HOI—Viet Cong defector.

CHINOOK—A twin engine helicopter large enough to take 60 combat troops in the air.

CLAYMORE—An anti-personnel mine that fires flechette razor sharp barbs. It has a killing zone of 50 to 60 meters from the point of detonation, in a 45 degree arc.

CO—A single Vietnamese woman.

CO CONG—A female Vietcong.

DEROS—The date and day that a soldier had completed his tour of duty and would leave for the States.

FIVE—Radio call sign for the executive officer of a unit.

FNG—Fucking new guy.

GARAND—The M-1 rifle which was issued to Vietnamese troops and used by the VC.

GREASE GUN—A 45-caliber automatic machine gun.

HE/HEAT—High explosive ammunition.

HELPER—A radio call sign for a combat battalion in the First Infantry Division. This unit operated for Divisional G-2 and G-5. It was made up of Chinese mercenaries, Philippine irregulars, Vietcong defectors, and various units of US troops and elements of the ARVN Fifth Division.

HOOTCH—Almost any shelter such as a tent.

HUEY/SLICK—Terms for the Bell UH-ID helicopter, the work-horse of Vietnam.

IN-COUNTRY—A term used to refer to US troops operating in South Vietnam.

KLICK—A thousand meters. A kilometer. Roughly eight-tenths of a mile.

LIMA/LIMA—Land line for telephone communications between two or more points on the ground. Also referred to as a Net.

LP—Listening post outside of friendly lines. Usually set up at night with two men and used to detect enemy activity.

LZ—Landing Zone. An area used for insertion or extraction of troops.

M-16—The standard infantry weapon of the Vietnam war, replacing the NATO M-14 during the years of 1966-67. It fired 5.56 ammunition, allowing the infantry to carry two to three times the amount of ammunition.

M-79—A short-barreled grenade launcher. It fires a 40mm shell about the size of a baseball. This included several types of functions, high explosive, white phosphorus, smoke canister, flechette, and buck-shot.

MACV—Military Assistance Command, Vietnam.

MEDEVAC/DUSTOFF—Medical evacuation or rescue by helicopter.

MP—Military Police.

NVA—The North Vietnamese Army.

PHU LOI BATTALION—A Vietcong regiment of about five hundred troops operating around Saigon.

PRC-10/PRC25—Referred to as the Prick 10, they were the standard infantry radio.

PUNGI—A sharpened bamboo stake hidden on trails to wound the enemy.

R AND R—Rest and relaxation from three to fourteen days. These leaves were taken in country in places like Nha Trang or outside like Japan.

REMIF—Rear echelon mother fuckers.

RF—Local military forces in a Province (State) and District (Country). Also called Rough Puffs, Kit Carson troops, Chieu Hoi (if troops were made up from former Vietcong), Hoi Chan, or Meows (troops from Central Highland Tribes).

RTO—The radio-telephone operator in a military unit.

RULES OF ENGAGEMENT—There were free fire zones such as jungle areas, limited zones such as French rubber plantations, restricted areas such as cities and Cambodian Border areas. So many civilians were killed that American troops operations in villages were followed by Division Staff Officers to pay the relatives for their relations that were killed if we could not prove them to be Vietcong.

SIX—Radio call sign for a unit commander.

SHORT/SHORT-TIMER—A person that has been in country close to a year and is getting ready to go back home.

TET—The Vietnamese New Year.

THREE—Radio call sign of the operations officer.

TWO—Radio call sign of the intelligence officer.

USAID—United States Agency for International Development. Used as a front for CIA operations.

VC—The Vietcong, also called Charlie, Vietnamese Communist.

WHITE MICE-ARVN—Military or Civilian Police.

WP—Willie Pete, or white phosphorus rounds used for marking targets. A cardinal rule to remember was that the shooter was also marking himself.

ZULU—Home radio base for a unit in the field.